LAND OF THE BRAVE

A C.T. FERGUSON CRIME NOVELLA (#2)

TOM FOWLER

WideningGyreMedia

Do you like free books? You can get the prequel novella to the C.T. Ferguson mystery series for free. This is exclusive to my VIP readers. Just go here to get your book!

Editing by Chase Nottingham.

Cover design by 100Designs

 Created with Vellum

CHAPTER 1

As was our tradition, my cousin Rich and I celebrated another closed case by hoisting a couple pints at a local tavern. This time, we chose the James Joyce Irish Pub in the Harbor East area of Baltimore. Rich honored our Irish ancestors by choosing a Guinness, and I honored them fifty percent more by ordering a Guinness Extra Stout. We sat at a table and sipped our festive brews.

"To another arrest," I said, raising my mug.

Rich tapped his to mine. "Hear, hear."

"You'll make lieutenant pretty soon at this rate." After doing the heavy lifting for my cases, I summoned Rich from the bullpen to make the arrests. He's a decorated detective with the Baltimore Police Department, a good bit earned on my cases.

"I'm doing all right on my own," Rich said. As usual, he refused to see the light on how much I'd helped his career in my ten short months as a private investigator. He'd been a plainclothes detective about the same amount of time and already earned more commendations than many of his longer-tenured colleagues.

"Now you've added a deadbeat dad to your ledger." I sipped again. Guinness Extra Stout—the beer that drinks like a meal.

"I was surprised you took the case at first." Rich smirked. "Then I saw the mom."

"Are you insinuating I only took the case because the client is attractive?"

"Attractive? She looks like a young Jennifer Connelly."

"I'm not old enough to remember a young Jennifer Connelly," I said. The ripe old age of twenty-nine stared at me from a couple months down the road. Rich had almost seven years on me. An occasional gray strand intruded on his otherwise brown crew cut. His hair was a couple shades lighter than mine, and I could boast of no gray. Rich maintained the hairstyle and clean shave as artifacts from his time in the Army.

"Watch *The Rocketeer* sometime," he said.

"I'll see if I can add it to my Netflix queue." Rich focused on his beer. I looked around the pub. It was a decent crowd for a weeknight with more diners than bar patrons. When I glanced back at Rich, he continued studying his beer as if something profound lay at the bottom of the glass. "You're quiet." Rich didn't answer. "Everything all right?" Nothing. I paused. "I just booked a trip to Mars."

"Mm-hmm."

"Rich." He frowned and looked up. "Something must be on your mind. You're silent and surly, even for you."

"I'm not surly."

"When you grumble, it kind of confirms it," I pointed out. Rich started to protest, but I broke in. "And don't tell me you weren't grumbling just now."

"Maybe a little," said Rich. Normally, he would have smiled or at least smirked. This evening, his expression remained neutral.

"What's up?"

Rich gazed at me for a second, then shook his head. "Nothing. Don't worry about it."

"Troubles with the ladies?" I said. Rich's expression didn't change. "You know, if you need advice from a younger, more handsome man, I'm willing to help."

"I do *not* need advice from you," Rich said.

"Rich, if this were still an era of little black books, you'd be stuck on page two." Now he scowled at me. "I, on the other hand, would be authoring a multi-volume epic."

"No one likes a braggart."

"Many of the names in my little black book would disagree," I pointed out.

"Whatever," he said. "Forget it."

I shrugged. "OK." After a few more swigs of my beer, Rich was just as chatty as before. I decided to give him some space this time. If he wanted to tell me, he would.

Rich looked at his beer some more, downed the rest in a giant swig, sighed, and looked at me. "Can we go to your office?" he said.

"Sure," I said. I paid the tab, and we left.

* * *

My office was an extra room in my house. I lived in an end-unit rowhouse in the Federal Hill section of Baltimore. Whoever owned it before me built an addition for the kitchen and turned part of the first floor into an office. It pinched the square footage of the dining room, but I usually ate in front of the TV, and I couldn't complain about the size of the living room.

I sat behind my desk. Three large computer monitors looked back at me. Rich took one of my guest chairs and busied himself looking around. This was not his first time in my office, and nothing in the room changed since his last trip. Still, I let him take his time and figure out whatever he wanted to tell me. The next time Rich confided in me may not be the first, but I could count them on one hand.

"You ever know my buddy Jim?" he said after a few minutes. "Jim Shelton?"

I shook my head. "Doesn't sound familiar."

Rich nodded and lapsed back into silence. A bad feeling welled in my stomach. I knew very few of Rich's friends, and chief among the reasons was Rich chose his friends carefully. Getting on the exclusive list amounted to a lifetime appointment. Whether I knew the man or not, if Rich mentioned one of his friends to me, I doubted the circumstances were good.

"He's dead," Rich said, confirming my suspicion.

"I'm sorry."

A nod again. "I'm sorrier for his widow and kids."

"Of course," I said.

I didn't say anything else. Rich needed time to unpack this and tell me about it. "Water?" I asked after a moment, reaching for the mini fridge.

"Sure."

I handed Rich a bottle, opened mine, and took a sip. Rich looked at his as if staring at it would compel the cap to open.

"Coroner says it's a suicide," he said.

A coroner involved meant it didn't happen around here. Baltimore, like most cities, had a medical examiner's office staffed with competent doctors. "I take it you don't agree."

"No way." Rich shook his head. "He wouldn't kill himself."

"You're certain?"

"Damn certain."

"Why?"

"We served together," Rich said. I presumed this; most of Rich's friends overlapped his years in the Army, especially the time spent in the Middle East. "When he got out, he . . . had some problems."

"PTSD?" I said.

"Yeah. I don't know if he ever got diagnosed or treated, but he had it."

Rich fell silent again. This time, I pushed on. "I don't mean to sound indelicate, but . . .

"It sounds like a suicide?" I gave the silent affirmative this time. "It does," Rich acknowledged. "But I know there's no way Jim would do it."

"How do you know?" I said.

"We talked about it some." Rich opened his water and took a long pull before continuing. "He admitted he thought about it. Even with a family, he still thought about it."

"What kept him from doing it, then?"

"An organization out there. Land of the Brave."

"Out there?"

"Garrett County," said Rich. The westernmost county in Maryland. Much of it was in the mountains in the panhandle of Maryland, and it offered short drives to both West Virginia and Pittsburgh. I hadn't been there in years and only for a weekend at Deep Creek Lake.

"How's the county doing?" I said.

"Not well. They've lost a lot of jobs. Jim had trouble finding work, and when he did, it usually didn't last long. He felt like he couldn't provide for his family after leaving them for years."

"I'm sure it was tough on him."

"It was." Rich drank more water and paused. I gave him the time he needed. "Land of the Brave got him a job, sort of."

"Sort of?"

"He worked with bees."

"Like a beekeeper?" I said.

"Yeah. He was responsible for several hives. They were set up on farms out there. The farmers leased out some land they weren't planting on anymore. Worked out for everyone."

"And this organization filled the land with bee hives?"

"I guess. Jim enjoyed the work. Said the buzzing didn't bother him. It let him focus. I think it was almost quiet for him." Rich frowned. "He told me working with the bees took a shotgun out of his mouth."

"Wow." I didn't have anything else to say, so I sat in my chair and stayed quiet.

"Yeah. I'm sure he didn't kill himself."

One of these days, I would need to get better at asking questions. I probably should have asked this one earlier. "How did he die?"

"Gunshot to the head," Rich said.

"It appears self-inflicted?" I said.

"Coroner's men found GSR on his hand."

"You think someone else shot him."

"Yes."

"So why would someone shoot an ex-Army guy with PTSD who's a beekeeper?"

"I don't know," Rich said, "but I want to find out."

"You want me to come along?" I said.

It took him a few seconds, and it was as small a movement a human could make to count as a nod, but I saw it. "I don't know if I can do everything myself," said Rich. "Besides, I'm too close to it."

"You're not going to gripe when I break into a database or thumb my nose at the law?"

"I'm off the clock."

"All right; I'll help you." I smiled. "Wow, you're hiring me. I should highlight this day on the calendar."

Rich smirked. It was good to see a positive reaction. "I think I regret it already," he said.

"No refunds."

"Good thing you work for free, then." Rich guzzled the rest of his water. "We'll leave in the morning. Can you be ready at eight?"

"Doubt it," I said. Rich glared at me. "It takes time to look this good. Not all of us have buzz cuts."

"Fine. You think you can finish primping and pampering by nine?"

"I'll manage."

"Good," Rich stood. "See you then. Anything you can find out in the meantime would be great."

"I'll see what I can put together," I said.

* * *

JAMES ALAN SHELTON died five days ago, three weeks shy of his thirty-eighth birthday. He left behind his wife Connie, ten-year-old James Junior, nine-year-old Carly, and two-year-old Patrick. Before Carly was born, the Army sent Jim to the Middle East, where he stayed a total of six years. Eighteen months later, he left the

Army and like so many veterans, struggled to adjust back to everyday life. Calling his post-service work history "spotty" would have asked the word to do work for which it was unqualified.

I pondered how far to dig. Normally, I threw caution to the wind and probed as deep as my considerable skill allowed. This case was more delicate. Not only was the victim a friend of Rich, he was also a veteran. I had no compunction using the Baltimore Police's resources for my own purposes or knocking over random databases. I didn't want to hack the Army. Even with good intentions, it felt wrong. I surprise myself with an attack of conscience from time to time.

During my first case, Rich left me alone at his desk for a few minutes, during which I snagged his IP and hardware addresses, then went home and used them to fingerprint the BPD's network. Ever since, their network has accepted one of my machines as its own. I could have used the BPD's resources to poke and prod the Army's network for more info on Jim Shelton. Doing so would have been lousy, though, and while my conscience rarely intruded, my feeling was Rich's I'm-off-the-clock proviso wouldn't extend so far.

Did I even need military records? Whatever Jim did in his tours of duty, he was several years removed. What were the odds someone tracked him to Garrett County and shot him? Rich and I were going up there to investigate. If we uncovered a tie-in to something related to Jim's service, I could go after the Army files then. Rich would probably approve at such a point, after the requisite moment of frowning and scowling.

Rich mentioned PTSD and the possibility Jim never had it diagnosed or treated. His comments were practically an invitation to snoop around the Department of Veterans Affairs and their databases. Never one to decline such an offer, I went about it. For an agency protecting gobs of sensitive information about the country's veterans, their network didn't present much of a challenge. A few minutes after discovering the VA's servers, I found one running an older version of Linux. One new exploit later, I was logged into it. From there, I moved laterally to some other servers, discovered a database administrator credential in a text file—this is unfortunately common—and looked for records on James A. Shelton. When I found them, I transferred them off the network, erased my tracks, and disconnected.

Since he got out, Jim had seen VA personnel on an irregular basis. I discovered a lot of rescheduled appointments, a few missed ones, and notes with a surprising lack of depth. It seemed Jim wasn't much of a talker, and the shrink he saw wasn't much of a speculator. Thus, no one ever made a formal diagnosis of post-traumatic stress disorder. The only treatment Jim received consisted of aperiodic appointments with a mediocre shrink and no medicine. I felt bad for Jim and his family, and at the same time, I hoped other veterans fared better.

Without much else to go on, I packed a bag for the next few days and went to bed.

CHAPTER 2

RICH ARRIVED PROMPTLY AT NINE THE NEXT morning. I don't think he'd ever been late for anything in his life. He was probably born right on schedule. I loaded my bag into the back of his blue Camaro, and we were off. Before we got on the highway, we stopped for coffee. I wanted to hit up the local java shop; Rich eschewed my choice for a Royal Farms because of its proximity to the on-ramp and (admittedly) better parking. Armed with extra caffeine, we got back into the car and headed west.

Oakland would be a three-hour drive. Rich got on I-83, which would take us to the Baltimore Beltway. From there, we would follow I-70 to I-68, and then Route 219 into Garrett County. Rich's navigation system directed him, but I knew he spent at least fifteen minutes last night studying a map—and a physical one to boot. If the Rand McNally corporation were to survive in this century of smartphones and GPSes, it would be on the backs of old folks and people like Rich. On the highway, we passed a few slower drivers and set a good pace. Like any sensible

Camaro owner, Rich opted for the powerful V-8 engine. Unfortunately, he paired it with the automatic transmission, for which I mocked him thoroughly after he bought the car. Rich tore up his left knee in the Army, though, so I understood his transmission choice. Despite this, I would still take some occasional jabs at him for it. What are cousins for? "How do you want to play this?" I said when we were on the Beltway.

"What do you mean?"

"Meaning, I know this guy was your friend, and you're the more experienced investigator."

"Nice of you to acknowledge it," Rich said.

"I didn't say you were the better one," I pointed out.

Rich chuckled. It was good to see his sense of humor make a comeback. "No need to say something so obviously true."

I let his comment go. It *was* true, even though I would only admit it under duress. "You want to talk to the family first?"

"No," said Rich. "Too much emotion there. I want facts first."

"Where do you want to start?"

"I've been reading the papers up there."

"They have newspapers in Oakland?" I said.

"The Garrett County *Republican*," Rich said.

"Well, it *is* a red county."

"They've picked up the story. It's become high-profile because of Jim's service."

"So you want to talk to the reporter?" I said. Rich nodded. "What about the cops?"

"Sheriff's Office, too," he said.

"You think they'll mind us snooping around?"

"They probably won't mind me too much. A

hotshot big-city PI like you, though, may not be too popular."

"I'll try to be fifteen percent extra charming," I said. "Good thing we're having more coffee."

"Just let me do most of the talking," Rich said.

We lapsed into silence for a few minutes. Rich guided the Camaro onto I-70 East. A short while later, the coffee was ready for post-processing by the ecosystem. We got off the highway and found a donut shop. After availing ourselves of the facilities, we each grabbed a couple donuts for the rest of the ride. I got a pair of French crullers. Rich, of course, opted for plain cake. Chocolate frosting was too much, and a honey glaze was right out.

"You bring a computer?" Rich said.

"Have we met?"

"I figured you would."

"I brought a good laptop and a router," I said. "You can't trust hotel and coffee shop wi-fi."

"Especially not for the kinds of things you might do," said Rich.

"You're the one who asked if I brought it. You're implicitly endorsing my methods."

"I'll have less of a problem with them on this case."

"I'm so glad you approve," I said.

Rich didn't say anything for a couple minutes. I was happy to listen to the classic rock playing on satellite radio. Then he said, "You're right. This is off the books. We need all hands on deck, and I'm glad you're coming along."

"Thanks," I said. "Was admitting it so hard?"

"Yes."

"Fair enough." I took a cruller out of the bag and bit

off a chunk of it. Two hours to go. I hoped most of them could pass in silence.

* * *

WITHIN THE CITY OF OAKLAND, Maryland Route 219 became Third Street. Despite its number, it served as the main drag. Oakland is not large, so its downtown is missing both the square footage and the bustle compared to a city like Baltimore. Only past the hospital did businesses and restaurants appear in volume with a Walgreens, McDonald's, Sheetz, and Pizza Hut in the span of a couple blocks. The *Republican* sat a block over on Second Street in a green building I would not have guessed housed a publisher. We parked out back and walked in through the front door.

Any newspaper still being operational in this day and age surprised me. The volume of people I saw when we walked in doubled my surprise. I expected a disenchanted skeleton crew trudging around amid dusty shelves and ancient computers. Instead, a receptionist smiled at Rich and me as we walked in, the people moving around behind her seemed happy to be at work, and the open floor plan looked modern. I couldn't see any computers—I still guessed them to be antiques—but everything else screamed modernity. The receptionist directed us to the second floor after Rich mentioned who we'd come to see.

On the upper level, the building showed its age. The open-concept seating of the first level didn't make it up here. Instead, people sat in a drab cubicle farm, the faded green fabric walls a poor callback to the building's exterior paint job. Offices were situated on the outsides of the cube area, and half of them empty, not even nameplates gracing their doors. The *Republican* put on a good show with the first floor, but the second story drove home the reality of the modern newspaper business.

We found our quarry on the left side. Luke Thompson was lucky enough to have a window seat, but unlucky to have a view of the parking lot. He was young, probably only a few years out of college, though his black hair was already thinning on top. He looked short and compact, built more like a fire hydrant than a news reporter. Maybe getting the scoop in Garrett County often involved fisticuffs. Rich and I each showed the reporter our IDs.

"Long way from Baltimore," he said with a hint of a southern accent.

"Just running down some leads," Rich said.

"You usually bring a private investigator with you?"

I liked this reporter. "I'm here to lend my unique expertise," I said before Rich could respond with something less impressive.

"What are you looking into?" he said. When Rich told him, Luke leaned back in his chair and let out a long, slow sigh. "That's not an easy one. You guys want some coffee?"

"Yes," I said.

"No," said Rich.

"I'll have the intern get us some from Sheetz."

"You have an intern?" I said.

"Surprised?"

"I'm surprised you have a newspaper. Everything else compounds it."

Luke smiled. "People still like getting a paper out

here. We're not all office drones glued to our phones and tablets."

The intern appeared when summoned, putting away his phone and appearing eager for work. He was tall and thin with red hair and a young face. He was probably in college but looked like he started shaving only yesterday. I could see the disappointment at fetching coffee darken his features, even when Luke offered to let him keep the change. After he left, Rich and I sat in extra chairs Luke found.

"Speaking of office drones glued to their phones," I said.

"Quincy is studying journalism at Frostburg," said Luke.

A name like Quincy would not help anyone, but I kept my thoughts to myself. There was a reason I went by my initials, after all. Rich filled in the brief conversational gap by saying, "Jim Shelton."

"Like I said, it's not an easy one."

"Meaning what?" I said.

"A decorated soldier kills himself. Always hard."

"You're convinced it was a suicide?" said Rich.

"Haven't seen anything to tell me otherwise," Luke said. "Gunshot wound looked self-inflicted, and he tested positive for residue on his hand."

"Doesn't mean it was a suicide."

"You know him?"

Rich nodded. "We served together."

"I'm sure it's tough to think he could kill himself."

"It's not tough," Rich said. "It's impossible. He wouldn't do it."

"Lot of guys in his place do," Luke said. "It's sad. This county isn't overflowing with jobs."

"He's not a statistic." I heard anger creeping into

Rich's voice. "Even without employment, he found a purpose. He found a reason to keep going."

To try and defuse any mounting tension, I broke in. "Land of the Brave."

"I've heard good things about them," Luke said. "They've made a difference."

"They made a difference for Jim Shelton, too," Rich said.

Quincy the intern returned with three cups of coffee. He set the tray on Luke's desk. A small bag held sugar and fake sweetener packets, a few plastic stirrers, and a pint of half-and-half. I took a cup and added a packet of sugar and enough creamer to turn the coffee a pleasing medium brown. Rich surprised me by using a packet of the yellow stuff. Under normal circumstances, I would have given him grief for it. Today, though, I didn't want to add to his tension. If anything, I wished he'd ordered a cup of decaf.

"You going to talk to them?"

"At some point, yes."

"If you need some notes on them, I could pass them along."

I sensed an ulterior motive here. "In exchange for what?" I said.

Luke grinned. "I can't just be a good guy?"

"You can. Maybe you are. All the same, you're a reporter, and I don't think you're volunteering a pile of information out of the goodness of your heart."

"Fine," he said. "I want the exclusive on whatever you discover.

"What if we discover it was definitely suicide?" I said. Rich glanced sidelong at me.

"Then I guess I'll have the scoop on the confirmation."

"Fine," said Rich.

We sipped coffee and chatted about a few local things with Luke. He recommended some places to eat —and others to avoid—and said he would send his notes along within a day. Rich and I walked out and got back in his car. "What's the plan now?" I said.

"Let's find a hotel," Rich said. "Then I want to talk to the sheriff."

I noticed his singular pronoun usage. "It sounds like you don't want me to come along."

"Probably best if you don't."

"What if I promise to simply sit there and look handsome?"

Rich smirked. "Can't have the sheriff threatened by your good looks," he said.

"Always a risk," I said.

* * *

Hotel options in Oakland were scarce. They were so deficient, in fact, as to be nonexistent. Rich and I chose the Oakland Motel. It was on the convenient side of the road if we needed to leave town in a hurry. The hospital and a few restaurants were short walks away. The motel featured brick exterior walls, dark blue doors, and a fridge and microwave in every room. Rich did not want to share a room with me—a sentiment I cosigned—so we ended with accommodations side-by-side. We paid the weekly rate in case the trip out here took a while.

"No wi-fi," Rich said as I put my bag on the bed.

"Doesn't matter," I said. "I brought a mobile hotspot."

"Couldn't someone figure out it's yours?"

I did my best to look insulted. "Rich. Really? Do you think I would set it up so there's any way to trace it back to me?"

"I suppose not."

"Go talk to the cops. I'll be here."

Rich left and closed the door. As I engaged the lock, I heard his Camaro rumble to life. Within a few minutes, I got the hotspot up and running and a fresh virtual machine on my laptop using it to talk to the outside world. I wondered how easy breaching the cyber defenses of the *Republican* would be. How much could a small-town newspaper put into keeping people like me at bay? It would also mean Rich and I could access Luke's notes even if he changed his mind and decided not to provide them. For now, I would leave them alone. Mostly. I poked and prodded their network, mapping out relevant devices and making my own notes.

From here, I could access the BPD's network. I wondered if they shared any info with the Garrett County Sheriff's Office and vice versa. Such a connection would be easy to exploit. Then I envisioned Rich with steam coming out his ears because I went and messed up the investigation. As amusing as I found the image of my strait-laced cousin as an angry cartoon character, I would respect his wishes. For now.

I passed the time doing research on Land of the Brave. They were a new organization in operation for about five years. The goal was to have veterans do productive work on farmland earmarked for the group to use. The most common work was beekeeping, and the organization sold and delivered the honey across the region and into West Virginia. In other cases, veterans grew other important crops for the area. Land of the Brave claimed to pay the veterans a stipend. They admitted it wasn't a living wage, but they hoped it would get there as more land and access became available. I always take charitable organizations with a grain of salt—my parents' foundation has encountered some charlatans over the years—but Land of the Brave seemed to be doing good, important work. If it saved veterans like Jim Shelton, it was even more important.

Why, then, had Jim killed himself? Or did someone murder him instead? I wondered if Rich learned anything during his chat with the sheriff. Think of the devil, and he shall arrive; the growl of Rich's Camaro announced his return. A minute later, he knocked on my door, and I let him in.

"What'd you learn?" I said.

"Some," said Rich. "Not enough for my tastes."

"You still think someone killed him?"

"We'll see. Put your shoes on."

"Why?"

"The mayor wants to talk to us," Rich said.

"Us?" I said.

"Yes. You, too, this time."

"Clearly my celebrity has spread."

Rich grinned and shook his head. "Yes, sir," he said. "Very good, sir. I have the car ready, sir."

"Well, it's about time," I said.

* * *

WE MET the mayor in an office in the circuit court building. He was tall and slender with blond hair and a goatee, and there was visible gray taking up about half the latter. He wore charcoal pants and a black sportcoat over a white button-down open at the collar. Small-town mayors could relax the dress code. He introduced himself as Ken Dennehy. His hands were large and his handshake grip strong. Rich and I sat across the desk from him. The mayor immediately insisted we call him Ken over anything more formal.

The office was small and sparse, the desk and three chairs occupying most of it. A meager bookshelf sat against the wall opposite the desk. It contained only a few law books, and they were as dusty as the shelves. Ken, as he wanted to be called, looked to be in his late forties. Based on the strength of his grip and the callouses I could feel on his hands, I pegged him as someone new to politics. "Terrible what happened to Jim," he said.

"You knew him?" Rich said.

"Oh, yes. Not close friends, I confess, but this isn't a big city. I know most people."

"How well did you know him?" I said.

"Enough to tell you he was a good guy in a bad spot. I thought he was going to pull through."

"You think he killed himself?" said Rich.

"Sheriff does," Ken said. "I don't see any reason to argue with him."

"Jim wouldn't kill himself."

"You friends?"

Rich nodded. "We served together."

"I had a feeling," the mayor said. "We need to do a better job for veterans coming home."

"Yes, you do," Rich said.

Ken frowned for an instant—as if he took it personally but wanted to hide the fact. "Land of the Brave does good work," he said. "I made sure they got a grant to give them enough funding to keep going."

"And dead veterans look bad for the city?" I said.

"That's an indelicate question."

"But a valid one."

Ken smiled, but I didn't see any humor in it. "I guess this isn't Baltimore," he said. "Of course it would look bad, but I'm a lot more concerned for Jim's family than I am for the city. The organization does good work. I'd give them the grant again." He paused. "Have you talked to his family yet?"

"No," Rich said. "Probably tomorrow."

"Why did you want to see us, Ken?" I said.

"To let you know I want you to succeed," he said. "Maybe there's a chance Jim didn't kill himself. I don't know. If there is, I hope you're able to work with our sheriff to figure out what happened."

"If we need some wheels greased along the way?"

"Then I'll try to be ready with the oil."

"Sounds good," Rich said. "Thanks."

The mayor shook our hands again. "Please keep me posted," he said, "and good luck."

In the car, Rich said, "You hungry?"

"Definitely."

"Let's find some food, then."

"And talk about what just happened," I said.

"You think something is weird?"

"I'm not sure," I said, "but I think better on a full stomach."

CHAPTER 3

Tomanetti's Pizza was an oddly-shaped building. Long rather than wide, its front door jutted out, and the brown roof didn't really go with the light red stone exterior. Inside, it fostered an old-time pizzeria feel with round brown tables and matching chair molding. Rich and I each ordered a pizza—pepperoni for him, mushroom and onion for me—and sat with our sodas. About half the tables were occupied, and a few people flittered in to pick up carry-out orders.

"You think something's up with the mayor?" Rich said. No one sat immediately around us, but Rich still possessed the good sense to talk in a quieter voice.

"I don't know," I said, shaking my head.

"He seems helpful."

"Yeah."

"However, you think that's weird?"

"It's a small city. He might know a lot of people, but he wasn't too close to Jim. Why talk to us, then?"

"Like you rather crassly said, dead veterans look bad for the city."

A sheriff's office car pulled up. A young deputy came in and looked around the restaurant. He picked up a pizza and went back to his car. "Dennehy's the mayor of Oakland," I said.

Rich shrugged. "And?"

"He's basically committing police resources to us. He's not the sheriff, and he's not the county executive."

"Do you know how many people live in the county?"

"I checked. Around thirty thousand."

"Right," said Rich. "More live in certain areas of Baltimore. You have a sparse population, not a lot of crime, and not a lot of out-of-towners asking questions."

"What's your point?" I said when he stopped talking without elaborating.

"In this kind of scenario, the mayor of the county seat could pull some strings. It's not like the deputies have a huge murder backlog."

"Maybe. I guess I'm just not used to people being helpful. Especially government people."

"Perhaps it's your typical charming approach," Rich said with a smirk.

Before I could fire off a clever retort, our pizzas arrived. They were cooked beautifully—as cooking shows would extol—with golden-brown cheese and the right amount of char on the crust. Tomanetti's didn't skimp on the toppings, either, and the amount of grease was exactly right. Rich and I put the conversation on hold as we each devoured three slices of pizza. We then got refills on our sodas and worked on fourth pieces.

"I think we're OK with the mayor," Rich said. "He most likely wants to help."

"I hope so," I said. "Let's see if we need the hand at some point."

"The sheriff already said his deputies would cooperate."

"You big-city cops and your fancy badges," I said.

"I'm sure cooperation's part of it. Remember, though, thirty thousand people in the whole county. The sheriff wants to help, too."

"Let me guess: he knew Jim."

Rich nodded. "Said he did, but like the mayor, not too well."

"I realize thirty thousand is a small population, but there's no way one man knows so many people. The president doesn't."

"I'm surprised you're so skeptical," Rich said.

"And I'm surprised you're not."

"What do you mean?"

"I'm here helping you out," I said. "Still for you, this is personal. You knew Jim well. He was your friend. People wanting to lend a hand is a good thing, but doesn't it all seem a little too easy?"

"I think you've watched too many movies. Different law enforcement agencies aren't always adversarial."

Rich certainly held the edge on me in experience. Plus, he worked in law enforcement, while I tried my damnedest not to get closer than the fringes. Maybe he was right. Dealing with unhelpful people in a city like Baltimore could have colored my perception. "OK," I said. "I'll follow your lead."

"But?"

"But if the mayor hires some slobbering goon to whack us over the head, I'm going to say I told you so."

"So noted," Rich said.

We both finished our sodas and got boxes to take the other halves of our pizzas back to the motel. Might as well take advantage of the limited amenities. "I want to stop and see Jim's family," Rich said after we were in the car. "At least talk to his wife."

"You want me to come in with you?"

"As long as you can turn off your conspiracy brain."

Rich pulled the Camaro back onto Route 219. He turned left before our motel and ended up on some twisty county road. Houses were infrequent, and the ones I saw were a mix of gracious Victorians and ramshackle ramblers. "Used to be nicer here," Rich said.

"Unemployment?"

"Big part of it. I think the rest is opioids."

"Even up here?" I said.

"You have a lot of people who worked hard jobs. A bunch of them needed painkillers. When they lost their jobs and insurance, they still wanted the pills."

"I guess it's everywhere."

"Yeah," Rich said. "It's even worse in West Virginia. We're not too far away." He paused. "See that house?" Rich pointed to a rundown small two-story building. Its current state of disrepair belied the fact it once served as a home. If a stiff breeze came along, I expected the structure to collapse. The roof had patches missing and beams exposed. What siding remained was worn and discolored. Most of the windows were gone, replaced with plastic sheets. The door was a large piece of ill-fitting plywood with a large X painted on it.

"What's the X mean?"

"It means first responders shouldn't go in. It's too unsafe, too likely to fall down."

"Do people live there?" I said.

"Doubt it," Rich said. "Sometimes, you get squatters. Often, people go there to do their drugs. Sometimes, they burn the house down, and the fire department doesn't run in."

I shook my head. Another house looking just as unsteady and with an identical X on the door appeared on the other side of the road. I wondered how many there were and how much longer they would still be standing. They threatened to slump to the earth any minute.

Rich made a right turn. The residences looked a little better here. No drug dens, at least. A deputy's cruiser drove past us and went down the road we just turned from. "Is this their street?" I said.

"Yeah, why?"

"Just wondering." *I don't have a conspiracy brain*, I told myself.

* * *

THE SHELTON PLACE looked like a log cabin. Two stories of wooden walls stopped at a traditional roof. None of the houses nearby looked like the Sheltons', nor did they look like each other. Absent anything like a homeowners' association, people built whatever dwelling they wanted and could afford. I liked the libertarian aspect, but looking between a white house, a blue one, a log one, and a rambler, I wished for some thematic unity.

Considering Jim's recent death, conditions of the lawn and gardens were understandable. Closer, I spied signs of age and disrepair—cracks in the logs, peeling paint on the door and shutters, and windows whose age exceeded mine. I wondered how many houses in the county met similar fates once jobs dried up.

Rich knocked on the door. A woman answered and invited us inside. In the living room, she and Rich embraced and exchanged words I couldn't hear. He introduced me to Connie Shelton, and we shook hands as I offered my condolences. Connie looked to be about Rich's age, though her eyes and the lines around them suggested she slept little in the last week. I heard children's voices from another room, but they didn't join us. Connie sat in a blue recliner; Rich and I shared a matching sofa.

The hardwood floors were the same color as the walls. They needed a good buffing to regain their luster. In light of Jim's passing, I tried to dial down my usual judgmental nature. Connie and the children faced other priorities. Floors could be maintained later. There would be time for dusting, cleaning, and putting toys away. I was sixteen when my older sister died; I didn't want to do much of anything afterward, and I wouldn't pretend my situation was the same as losing a husband.

"Thanks for coming." Connie mustered a small smile. "Both of you. Can I get you anything?"

"We're good," Rich said. "Tell me what's happened."

Connie let out a slow sigh. " Oh, dear . . . after Jim died, the coroner did an examination. The sheriff and some deputies came around. They talked to me, talked to the kids some. I hear they went out to the farm and questioned the charity people, too."

"Did anything come of it?"

"No." Connie snorted without humor. "Single gunshot wound to the head. No sign of foul play, the coroner says. No motive for someone to kill Jim, the sheriff says. So they tell me he killed himself." She shook her head as a single tear slid down her right cheek. "I don't believe it."

"I don't believe it, either," Rich offered.

"What are you going to do?" Connie said.

"We'll look around, talk to people, and dig into what happened."

"You think you can figure out who killed Jim?"

"Yes," Rich said right away. I thought odds were good of doing it, but I also didn't want to promise results to a recent widow.

Connie looked at me. "You're Rich's cousin?"

"I am."

"You're not a cop?"

"Private investigator," I said. Describing myself this way for almost a year, it got easier to say, yet it still felt weird to hear myself say it.

"You must be good, if Rich brought you here to help."

"I tend to get results." Rich shifted beside me. I couldn't see his face, but I knew he must have been frowning.

Connie picked up on it. "Is something wrong?"

Rich's response was probably best for everyone. "I don't want to sit here and ask you a bunch of questions," he said.

"I think you know the answers."

"I probably do, but I'm a cop, and Jim deserves my thoroughness. Had anything been unusual lately?"

"No," Connie said. "I think working with the bees was helping Jim. It'd probably drive me batty, but it seemed to calm him down. He was in a better place in his head these last couple months."

"He got along with everyone?"

She nodded. "Charity people were great. Farmer was really nice. I think he was glad someone could use the land."

"Did he have any quotas with respect to bees or honey?" I asked.

"You think someone killed him 'cause he didn't make enough honey?" Connie said.

"People have been killed for less."

She paused to think about my question. "If he had any goals to hit, he never mentioned them to me. It didn't seem like that kind of place. Sure, they could sell the honey, but it ain't like honey sells for fifty bucks a jar."

Her point was valid.. Even if Land of the Brave sold their honey at high-end prices—presuming Garrett County and West Virginia shoppers would pay those rates—they'd need millions of bees to bring in a lot of money. Giving a handful of veterans a few hives each wasn't a formula to hoard cash and retire young.

"We'll figure it out," Rich said to reassure Connie.

I refrained from joining in the affirmation. Even though I liked our chances, nothing about this case made me think we would have an easy go of it.

* * *

"Now YOU'RE QUIET," Rich said as he drove us out of the neighborhood.

"Am I surly, too?" I said.

"Surly suits me more than you."

I fell silent for a moment before saying, "This is a small city and a county with a low population."

"So?"

"So everybody knows everybody else. People are aware of their neighbors' lives; they know their business."

"I still don't understand what you're getting at," said Rich.

"I mean, obviously Jim's wife is going to think he

didn't kill himself. What if he hid something from her, though? Something we might find out by asking around?"

"You think he killed himself?" Rich's voice took on an edge.

"I'm trying to keep an open mind. If he got killed, though, someone did it for a reason. He may not have told his wife about it."

"But you think he may have told someone else."

"Yes," I said.

"Maybe. The problem is everyone knows everyone here."

"What do you mean?"

"Because they don't know you," Rich said. "They don't know me. We're outsiders. They're going to protect their own."

"I guess." We got back onto Route 219 for the short jaunt to the motel. "It may be worth trying."

"Let's see how tomorrow goes first."

Rich turned into the motel parking lot. One vehicle we hadn't seen before, a gray SUV, sat near our doors. As we pulled closer, four large men got out of the SUV and took up positions near the doors. "The welcoming committee," I said. "Still think everyone we've talked to has been helpful?"

Rich gave me a sidelong glare as he parked his Camaro in a spot two down from the goonmobile. "We can't be sure who sent these guys."

"Why don't we find out?" I said as I got out.

Rich called, "C.T.!" after me, but I closed the door. He got out, too. The two men standing near my door sized me up. Both crossed their arms under their chests, and those arms and chests were bigger than mine. All of them stood about six-four, giving them two inches on me and four on Rich. They were built like offensive linemen, so I didn't doubt their strength even as I noticed their unnecessary bulk and paunches.

"You from the local Four-H?" I said as I stopped a couple paces from the pair darkening my doorstep.

"What the hell is a four-aych?" the one on the right said. His long black hair was pulled back into a pony-tail. The other one wore his blond hair in a super short buzz cut even Rich would have found severe.

"Hell, I don't know." I thought about it for a second as they looked between each other, then scowled at me. "Head, heart, health . . . you know, I forget the fourth one."

"We ain't from the fucking Four-H," the blond one said.

"I believe you," I said. "They'd never approve of your language."

"Who sent you?" Rich said, plopping a wet blanket atop the banter I had going.

"You two assholes are asking too many questions," one of the two by Rich's door said.

"Right now," I said, "I just want to know what the fourth H stands for."

"You need to back off," Black Ponytail said. "Go back to Baltimore."

"Or what?" I said.

"Or we'll send you there in an ambulance."

"Why would it take us back to Baltimore? There's a hospital around the corner."

"Enough of this shit," Blond Crew Cut said as he grabbed for me. I shoved his arm aside and gave him a short jab in the solar plexus. Sucking wind made him take a step back into the wall. Behind me, I heard the telltale grunts and sounds of fighting as Rich's duo failed to persuade him to leave. The goon with the black ponytail threw the kind of loopy hook a boxing teacher would expel someone for. I blocked it. He lobbed a few more. They were strong but but slow and gave me time to turn all the blows aside.

My blond assailant recovered and pushed himself off the wall. This could get complicated. When Black Ponytail launched his next haymaker, I grabbed his arm and spun him into the parking lot. His momentum carried him into the front quarter panel of the gray SUV, from which he bounced and fell in a heap. I turned back toward Blond Crew Cut in a defensive stance.

He threw a hard jab at my face. I pushed his punch high with my left arm, ducked a bit, and rammed my fist into his stomach. When he bent forward, I drew back my arm and walloped him in the face with an elbow. His head rebounded off the door and his eyes crossed. I did it again, then a third time, until he slumped down the door.

The long-haired goon got to his feet as I waded out to meet him. Out of the corner of my eye, I saw Rich deliver a knockout blow to one of his attackers. "I just remembered what the fourth H is," I said.

"Huh?" he said.

"Hands." I launched a flurry of punches at his body. He managed to turn a few aside, but the majority connected. He rocked back with the impacts and his breathing grew labored. I gave him one last good shot to the midsection, then grabbed his ponytail and bashed his head into the hood of the car. When the first attempt didn't put him down, I did it again. The second one turned the lights off.

Both of Rich's assailants were flattened, too. His

split lip leaked a little blood down his chin. "I think my two were bigger," I said, eying the four men splayed out around the motel doors and parking lot.

"I don't think so," said Rich.

I pointed at the one with the ponytail. "He's got more hair."

Rich chuckled and shook his head. "Not everything is a competition."

"Good thing," I said, touching my lip in the spot where his was busted open.

Sirens screamed from nearby. I saw red and blue flashing lights as three sheriff's cars drove into the lot and skidded to stops near the scene. One deputy stepped out and pointed his gun at us.

"They started it," I said as I raised my hands.

CHAPTER 4

Rich and I rode to the sheriff's office in separate police cars. Once we established he was a police detective and I was a private investigator, the deputies decided not to handcuff us. Ambulances took the four attackers turned victims to the nearby hospital. They never told us who sent them. I wondered if the deputies would have any idea and if they would tell us anything they knew.

The Garrett County Sheriff's Office was in the same building housing the district and circuit courts and where Rich and I met the mayor. I got the feeling Ken Dennehy wouldn't be chatting us up tonight. The deputies herded Rich and me inside. The squadroom looked like it had been lifted straight out of 1990s cop dramas and deposited here. Desks loosely organized into rows butted against one another. The vinyl floor was pockmarked with coffee stains. Whiteboards filled with active cases and other official scribblings covered most of the available wall space. Doors to offices and interrogation rooms ringed the exterior.

A tubby deputy led me to one of those enclosures,

pointed at my chair, and left without saying a word. If it came down to running away, I liked my chances against him. I would be back at the motel before the ambulance arrived to tend to his coronary. The interrogation room was just as unspectacular as the rest of the area. Paint peeled from the walls in a few spots. I sat on a plastic chair whose design specifications clearly listed comfort at the bottom. The seating reserved for my inquisitor boasted a thin layer of padding covered by gray cloth—probably not much more comfortable. The required one-way mirror dominated the wall to my right. I waved in case anyone watched from the other side.

Then I waited. And I waited some more. If the Garrett County Sheriff's personnel sought to turn me into a quivering mass of gelatin by waiting me out, they would be disappointed. I used the downtime to ponder recent developments in the case. Rich and I talked to few people, yet we still had a quartet of legbreakers greeting for us. No one called 9-1-1, but deputies came anyway. Someone at the motel could have sounded an alarm, but the parking lot was mostly empty. The office was too far away to have a good view of the scrum, and the units didn't have exterior cameras. Right after the law arrived, an ambulance rolled into the lot. The whole thing smelled like a setup to me. It caused me to wonder who would have sent the four idiots to dissuade us, and would the same person have had first responders on standby?

Of course, someone trying to encourage us to abandon the investigation meant there was something to investigate. No one should care about extra scrutiny on a suicide. A murder, though, could not withstand a glut of questions, especially not when posed by someone as brilliant as me. Rich, too, for that matter.

Whatever room Rich sat in, I felt certain the same thoughts came to him. We were onto something, and whoever was responsible didn't want us to stay on it. I also wondered if some deputy would come in and suggest we abandon this and go back to Baltimore.

A few minutes later, a middle-aged deputy entered the room. Unlike the fat one who showed me in here, this man looked like he could still play a mean left field in a softball league. His hair had gone gray, but he looked to be about my height and build—six-two and about 185 pounds. His name tag identified him as White, and he was. So, too, would his hair be in another ten years. He set a manila file folder and a small spiral notebook on the table in front of him as he slid into the chair. "You know why you're here?"

"I'm extremely good at defending myself?" I said.

"You put two men in the hospital."

"There you go." His neutral expression told me he was unconvinced. "They would have done the same to me."

"But they didn't," White said.

"Do you really think my cousin and I picked a fight with four guys their size?" I said.

White shrugged. "Couple of hotshots from Baltimore . . . don't know what kind of trouble you'd start."

"You might look at the quartet we laid out. I doubt they're as pure as the driven snow."

"Now you're going to tell me how to do my job?" said White.

"Only because it appears someone needs to," I said.

My comment made White glare at me. I didn't wilt. He moved the notebook aside and opened the folder. Inside, I saw a few sheets of paper. The picture on the top page looked like one of the goons I tangled with.

"We already did that," he said. "I guess someone else told me how to do my job before you. All four of these guys are dirty." White leafed through the pages. The print was small, and I was reading upside-down, but it looked like two of the men hailed from West Virginia.

"Local boys?" I said.

"Mm-hmm. They seem to specialize in the work you saw them doing tonight. We've arrested all of them before."

"Yet I'm the one in this room," I pointed out.

White raised both hands and slapped the tabletop hard. I didn't flinch, though I wondered if the rickety table would survive. Before I worked my first case, I lived in China for thirty-nine months, culminating with nineteen days in one of their prisons. It was an experience I did not care to repeat, but it made me immune to amateur tactics like the one White used. "What did this poor table ever do to you?" I said.

"You're a smart ass."

I was about to say I preferred it to being a dumbass but refrained. White seemed competent and didn't deserve the barb. When did I go soft? "The key word is 'smart,'" I said instead.

"All right, let's presume you're smart. What are you and your cousin doing up here?"

I figured White knew this already, but I played along. "Looking into the death of Jim Shelton."

"Suicide," said White.

"The four men trying to get us to drop our inquiry would disagree," I said.

"Yeah? Why?"

"Real suicides stand up to scrutiny. Murders dressed up to look self-inflicted can't take the spotlight for long."

"You think someone killed Jim Shelton?"

"I was on the fence until we got the welcoming committee at our motel."

White lapsed into silence. He busied himself looking through the papers again. With another chance to eye the reports, I confirmed seeing West Virginia on two sheets. Perhaps the talent market for legbreakers was at low ebb in Garrett County. "Say you're right," he said, and I resisted the urge to say I was right. "Who killed him?"

"We don't know yet," I said, "but I guess whoever sent four assholes to our rooms is a likely suspect."

"You know who did it?"

I shook my head. "None of them said much except the usual threats."

"Maybe you could have given them more of a chance to talk."

"Sure. I'll just get punched around a bit to help your nonexistent investigation." I pointed at my face. "Can't risk the money maker."

"I did some asking about you," White said. "Talked to a Captain Sharpe in Baltimore."

"Leon is a big fan," I said.

"He told me you're a self-impressed rogue with no regard for process."

"He sometimes couches his fandom in tough talk."

White said, "OK, he did also say you're smart and tenacious."

"I told you. He has a foam finger with my name on it."

"Just make sure you keep us in the loop."

"You're not going to investigate?" I said.

"It's been ruled a suicide," White said. "I get your

point about the guys coming to visit you, but that's not enough to reopen the case."

I preferred them staying out of it. Rich and I were more likely to find the truth unencumbered by the deputies' investigation. "I'm sure we'll keep you informed," I said.

"Be sure you do. We can haul you in here again. Having a chat with the mayor won't save you from an obstruction charge."

So the sheriff's office, or at least White, knew about our talk with Ken Dennehy. Interesting.

"Noted," I said.

* * *

Rich and I sat in my motel room after the deputies let us go. I sat on the bed. If lounging on it proved any indication, a mediocre night of sleep awaited me. Rich was parked in an office chair. The room lacked a desk but still featured a padded chair with arms and wheels straight out of cubicle farms. I wondered if it was more comfortable than the bed.

"They grill you much?" I said.

"Not really," said Rich. "They asked why I was here, why I brought you along, why I thought Jim was murdered." He shrugged. "Pretty basic. You?"

"The deputy I talked to didn't seem impressed to share the interrogation room with a 'Baltimore hotshot,' as he called me."

"Did you set him straight?"

"To whatever degree I could," I said. "I still wonder who called nine-one-one."

"Probably someone here," Rich said.

"Look at the parking lot. Three other cars, and none within a few doors of our rooms."

"You think it was a setup of some kind." It wasn't a question.

"I just wonder."

Rich fell silent. Maybe he ruminated on it, too. After a moment, he said, "I want to visit the charity tomorrow."

"What do you think we'll find?" I said.

"I don't know. Hell, there's a lot of unknowns since we got here. Maybe I'm hoping we'll find some clarity."

"I might settle for a couple shady dudes giving us the side-eye."

Silence again served as the only reply I got. Rich stood and pushed the corner of the drab curtain back. He peered out the window.

"Thinking we might have more visitors?" I said.

"I wish I could put a finger on what to expect," said Rich. He still looked out into the parking lot. "Did the deputy believe you about Jim?"

"I think so."

"Same here. Did he say they'd do anything?"

"I doubt it," I said. "He mentioned it's still officially a suicide, so until that gets overturned, they're not investigating."

Rich let go of the curtain and sat back down. "I heard pretty much the same thing. No one even suggested they would talk to the coroner." He shook his head. "I wish this county employed a medical examiner."

"The coroner could be good at his job."

"Maybe," Rich said. "But he's elected . . . in a county where a lot of people know each other. He stays popular, he can keep getting elected even if he doesn't know a scalpel from a hatchet."

"We could always pay him a visit," I suggested.

"No." Rich shook his head. "I'd rather work around him. Let's figure out what happened. Then we'll drop the evidence on the sheriff's desk and make him act."

I hoped it would be enough. "I'm with you," I said.

CHAPTER 5

Land of the Brave served Garrett County, Allegheny County, and parts of West Virginia from its office near Deep Creek Lake. It was about fifteen minutes outside of Oakland. The area was home to a ski resort, plenty of camping, and a more upscale feel than anywhere else in the County. It seemed a curious place for a nonprofit to make its home, but here was Land of the Brave. They operated from their own building, a single-story structure whose shape suggested it was a restaurant in a past life.

The parking lot butted against Route 219. A sign in the lot simply read "Land of the Brave." No signage or other information showed on the building itself. It featured beige siding, a couple bay windows, and a large ovular door bisecting the exterior. We walked past one of the windows. Inside, a few people sat at desks. Rich and I entered. The receptionist, a pretty blonde girl who looked like she still had a couple years to go at Frostburg State, smiled and greeted us.

"Are you veterans?" she said.

"I am," said Rich.

"Thank you for your service. Do you need some help?"

"We do." He showed his badge. Not to be outdone in the presence of an attractive girl, I flashed my ID. "I think we need to talk to your boss."

"Is this about the poor man who killed himself?" she said.

"Yes," I said when Rich didn't answer. He shot me a sidelong glance. I frowned in return. What was the benefit of keeping those details on the down-low?

"Sure," the receptionist said. She walked past us to the other side of the building. Everything was laid out with an open floor plan save for one office. It was obviously built after the rest of the place. It looked like someone hurried like mad to hang the drywall and sacrificed professionalism for haste. Whoever painted it displayed the same work ethic. Maybe corners like good construction needed to be cut to afford the square footage near the lake. Rich and I waited. A moment later, the girl returned. "You can go in."

The office looked no better on the inside. The painter did just as shoddy a job there. I could not claim painting expertise—my next time taking up a roller would be the first—but uneven applications and bad corner work are easy to spot. A few pictures dotted the walls, mostly of men in uniforms of the five service branches . The desk the director sat behind looked as hastily assembled as the walls surrounding him. He stood and fixed us with a neutral expression. No nameplate was on his desk, but the degree hung behind him —a bachelor's from West Virginia University—identified him as Peter Russell.

"How y'all doin'?" he said. I heard traces of an accent my amateur ear would place as hailing from

Tennessee. Russell looked a shade under six feet and quite a bit over 200 pounds. His shaved head made his age tough to guess, but I went with mid-forties. The office was about the size of an extra bedroom in a townhouse, with just enough room for Russell's desk, a couple shabby guest chairs, and a small round table and shopworn loveseat.

"Detective Ferguson," Rich said, giving a businesslike reply while showing his badge.

"And Detective Ferguson," I said, taking out my ID.

"All the way from Baltimore," Russell said as he looked at Rich's shield. A smirk briefly crossed his face, like he knew Rich enjoyed no jurisdiction so far from the big city.

"Jim was my friend," Rich said. "We served together."

"We were all sorry to hear what happened to him."

Rich and I sat in the guest chairs. Russell showed us a smile, but any warmth it held didn't reach his eyes. "Terrible thing," he said. "It's always a shame when we can't reach someone."

To his credit, Rich didn't take the bait. He stayed focused on his questions. "Can you tell me what your organization does?"

"Glad to. We work with veterans. You said you served?" Rich nodded; Russell continued. "You found a good job for yourself. A lot of the ones who come back aren't so lucky."

"I know."

"I'm sure you do. What we do is work with the ones who have problems adjusting to life once they're home. Usually, that's trouble finding a job."

"You don't offer counseling?" said Rich.

"We make referrals," Russell said, "if we feel someone needs help beyond the VA."

"Did Jim Shelton?"

"He was talking to a psychologist we helped him find, yes."

"Recently?" I said. Russell inclined his head. This shrink must not have interfaced with the VA because Jim's records didn't mention any recent visits. "Do you know how his therapy was going?"

"We don't get involved on that end," Russell said. "It'd be a legal issue for us. The therapists do their work, and we do ours."

"So you never hear from them?"

"Their offices let us know if they pick up a patient we referred. We don't ask for anything else."

"Did Jim talk to you or anyone here about how it was going for him?" Rich asked.

"Here and there," said Russell. "He said he found a good medication. We thought he was doing well."

"What about his job?"

"Yes. He was an excellent worker. We gave him a couple choices of what to do. He tried working with the bees once and really took to it. Lotta guys don't even attempt it." Russell paused. "It's consistent work. You're doing the same things a lot. Very . . . rote, if you will. Jim loved it. I think the buzzing sound was good for him, too. He mentioned that he actually found it soothing."

"What did he do?" I said.

"Honey. He checked on the health of the bees and the hives, of course. But he also processed honey, bottled it, and boxed up cases. We take it to local markets and sell it. Organic raw wild honey."

"Very Whole Foods-y," I acknowledged. I'd bought the identical product before.

"Well, we don't have a lot of stores like that up here," Russell said, giving us a brief grin. "But the markets we do have are happy to sell what we give them. Now, we take it to West Virginia, and you get some different stores down there. Even a Whole Foods or two."

"Anything else besides honey?" Rich said.

"Our company leases land from farmers. Most up here don't use all their fields anymore, so they're glad to take money from us. We're limited in what we can do. Honey is a popular seller, so we're looking to gather more by placing hives for pollinating some crops and orchards and keeping the honey. We also grow some fruits and vegetables, and sell bags of topsoil."

"You pay the veterans?" I said.

"What we can," said Russell. "They get a basic stipend, plus a cut of whatever gets sold out of their lots."

Rich said, "So the more they produce, the more they can make."

Russell spread his hands in a modest gesture. "Exactly. It's not as much as a good full-time job, but we do what we can. Cost of living is pretty low up here."

I figured it was quite a bit cheaper in Oakland or border towns in West Virginia than by Deep Creek Lake but didn't bring it up. I didn't want to antagonize Russell. At least not yet. "What about housing?" Rich said.

"What about it?" Russell said.

"You said cost of living is cheap. I've driven around. It's an interesting mix, but there are definitely some not-so-nice ones out there. Do you help people find better accommodations?"

"We haven't yet, I admit. No one has asked. Obviously, we don't want anyone living in squalor. We're not going to butt in, though. People need to learn to ask for help."

"About Jim," Rich said. "His wife is convinced he didn't kill himself."

Russell said, "I don't mean to sound indelicate, but don't wives normally think so? You're a cop in a city with a lot more crime than we get out here. You see many families who agreed with a determination of suicide?"

He drove home a point. I was on Team Rich here, but Russell's statement was valid. Families rarely believed their loved ones were capable of suicide. Even when signs of depression were copious and obvious, disbelief was common. Denial, after all, was the first stage of grief. "Families never agree," Rich confirmed, echoing my thoughts. "Sometimes, they're deluding themselves. Other times, they're right."

"You think they're right here?"

"I do. Jim wouldn't kill himself."

"I'm sorry, Detective. Deputies investigated. The coroner ruled it a suicide."

"I'm here to make sure they didn't miss anything," Rich said. "It was less than a week ago."

"They know you're here?" Russell said.

"Why?" I said. "You going to call them and narc on us when we drive away?"

Russell put his hands up again, this time in defense. "I don't want to see you get hauled off because you're concerned about your friend."

Rich smiled. In profile, it looked just as sincere as Russell. "We've talked," he said.

"Good. I wish you gentlemen good luck, then."

We didn't have any other questions, so we left. Rich stewed all the way back to the motel. I didn't try to talk to him. He needed space and time to process everything, and I wanted to look into Land of the Brave and Peter Russell.

* * *

FREE WI-FI IS A MINEFIELD. People gleefully connect all manners of devices to unsecured networks. If they knew the information a fellow like me could pilfer in only a few minutes, they would wait to look at their cat pictures and political memes. Even an average hacker—and I am well above average—can get login details, passwords, and personal info in short order. The motel didn't offer wi-fi, but my laptop found other networks nearby. Unsecured, of course. Hard pass.

With no wireless I trusted, I hunted around for a wired connection but never found one. Good thing I brought the mobile hotspot. It was a couple years old, but it offered a reliable 4G connection no one could trace back to me. I interfaced it with the router and joined the network. Stage one, complete. I was too paranoid to have one simple layer of protection, however. After obtaining an IP address, I launched a virtual private network. Companies use VPNs so remote workers can connect to the corporate network securely even over the public Internet. Some free ones are out there, but I used a paid service offered by some acquaintances.

After establishing a session with the VPN, I then

used an anonymizer to further hide my traffic. With three layers of security in place, I got to work. Land of the Brave had been around for six years. Three years ago, they moved from the second story of a building in downtown Oakland to their current location. Moreover, the organization didn't have increased revenues corresponding with the move. Money earned from selling their products followed a gradual upward trend, but I saw nothing to indicate they could soak up what I presumed to be twice the rent with no problems. So I dug deeper.

I expected Land of the Brave to use WordPress for their website like so many others. Instead, they had their own web server running Apache. Luckily for me, they missed the last couple Apache updates. Any outdated software is vulnerable. A simple search showed me an exploit. A minute later, I had it loaded and ready, and once sixty more seconds elapsed, I gained unfettered access to the server. Their site wasn't bad. Like most small companies, however, their web server got forced into service in other areas. It also operated as their file server.

I poked around for a few minutes and ended up copying everything. Nothing else looked interesting enough to pilfer. I covered my electronic footprints and disconnected. The files were mostly boring. I downed two cups of coffee at breakfast, and fifteen minutes with this information left me yearning for a third.

Nothing in the personnel records raised a red flag. The organization kept data on all the veterans it helped; I ignored all of them except for Jim Shelton's. If we needed to, Rich and I could go back and pore over them later. For now, I wanted to preserve their privacy. I took a small portable printer out of my bag and put the information to paper. I knew Rich would prefer reading a hard copy.

My phone rang a few minutes later, offering me a reprieve from this tedium. Gloria Reading called. If Baltimore could be said to have socialites, Gloria would be first among them. She and I enjoyed a relationship of fun and convenience. Her parents and mine moved in the same social circles, though Gloria enjoyed those circles more than I did. "You're a hard man to find," she said when I answered. I heard the playful edge in her voice and imagined the lascivious look often on her face.

"I'm out of town with Rich," I told her.

"I didn't think you guys were the type to go away together."

"We're not." Gloria knew me well enough to know Rich and I were a distant sort of close. "Rich wanted my help with something."

"Wow. That's a big step, isn't it?"

"I guess it is," I said. "One of Rich's friends from the Army died. It's been ruled a suicide. We came out here to . . . make sure the investigation was good." Even though we knew it probably wasn't.

"I'm sorry for Rich," Gloria said. "Did the man have a family?"

"Yes."

"That's terrible." She paused. "Is there anything I can do?" A few months, maybe even thirty days ago, Gloria wouldn't have asked. When we first met, I think she found the idea of me working quaint in some way. In an ideal world, I wouldn't have needed to, but I blew my money bankrolling my hacker friends when I lived in Hong Kong. Nineteen days in a Chinese prison later, I was back in the States and the object of my parents' ire. They wanted me to get a job helping people; I wanted to work as little as possible. We soon found common ground: I would work for their foundation and solve cases pro bono. Over time, Gloria took an interest in my work. She had even come with me on some of the more social outings my cases required.

"I doubt it," I said. "I'd suggest you come ski at Wisp, but it's not really the season yet."

Gloria chuckled. "I'm not much of a skier."

"Neither am I."

"You've had some dangerous cases recently," she said. "Is this going to be another one?"

"I hope not," I said, "but I wonder. It seems like the police are watching Rich and me. He thinks I'm paranoid. Maybe I am. Already, a few guys tried to stare us down and dissuade us."

"What happened?"

"They weren't very good at the dissuading part."

"Be careful, C.T."

"Sounds dangerously like concern," I said with a grin I couldn't help.

"I don't want to see anything happen to you," said Gloria. "I . . . enjoy our time together."

"So do I."

"When do you think you'll be back?"

"I don't know. I hope no more than a few days."

"Make sure you get here in one piece," Gloria said in a sultry voice. Even through the phone, it sent a shiver down my spine.

"I'll do my damnedest," I said.

* * *

RICH CAME by about an hour later. This time, I sat on the desk, laptop in its eponymous place, and Rich took the bed. "I heard you on the phone earlier," he said. "Gloria?"

"Yeah."

"When are you gonna marry that girl?"

I snorted. "Rich, come on. I like Gloria, but I'm not sure either of us are the marrying types."

"You two are fooling yourselves," he said with a grin.

"I hope you didn't come over here to give me relationship tips," I said.

"No," he said. "Just wondering if you did any work while you weren't busy talking to your girlfriend."

I was about to point out Gloria wasn't my girlfriend. Rich's smirk changed my mind. Let him have his satisfaction. "I have, in fact. Something Russell said troubled me."

"What was it?"

"When he said Jim was seeing a psychologist and had tried some medication." Rich shrugged. "Psychologists can't prescribe. They're not medical doctors."

"Interesting," said Rich. "Do you know where the prescription came from?"

"I haven't looked yet. His comment got me thinking the organization wasn't so pure. I've been nosing around."

"And?"

"I'm not an accountant," I said. "Thank goodness. But I don't know how they afford their building and all the employees. They show six full-time and eight part-timers. Their current office is more than double the rent at the old one."

"Donations?" Rich said.

"They get some, sure. Not as much as I would expect, and they only make money selling honey and other small things, while ignoring a more lucrative pollination business. It doesn't add up."

"What about Russell himself? He could have money and run the whole thing at a loss."

"Maybe," I said. "I'm going to look into him next. In the meantime, I printed some things for you."

Rich grabbed the small stack of papers. "Let me know what you find about Russell," he said.

"I'm on it. I'll know all the things worth knowing about him soon." I fired up the VPN and anonymizer again. It was time to see what skeletons Pete Russell crammed into the dark corners of his closet.

CHAPTER 6

PETER RUSSELL CAME FROM A LARGE FAMILY. HE was the fourth of eight children. Six of his seven siblings were still alive. Unless any of them hit the lottery, their ages indicated they would still be working. They were. A few minutes of searching found them scattered throughout the east coast and Midwest. All of them had boring jobs that didn't interest me for this case.

Except one.

George Russell was an administrator at the Fairmont Regional Medical Center, named for the city in which it's located in West Virginia. I couldn't count Fairmont among the two cities in West Virginia I'd heard of—Morgantown and Harpers Ferry—so I looked it up. Driving there from Oakland would take about ninety minutes. A regional hospital would have access to all manners of drugs. George could hook up Pete and his shrink with some. I hypothesized this was how Jim Shelton got his medication.

A quick job search told me the salary I could expect to earn as a candidate for hospital administrator jobs. I then poked around until I found where George Russell did his banking and investing. My degree is in computer science, so I'm pretty good at math. Even if I weren't, though, I could have deduced something fishy in George's books. Unless he'd been working for about fifty years—almost quadruple the length of his current career—he couldn't have saved and stashed all the money he did.

I looked deeper. George's paycheck hit his savings every two weeks. He also made small cash deposits once a month, as well as large investments in his brokerage account around the same time. Another savings stash showed irregular cash deposits and ATM withdrawals. If I didn't know better, I'd think George was a drug dealer.

Hospitals received medications all the time. Some were boring, like aspirin and Tylenol, and even though you could buy a bottle of them for three dollars, the hospital would still charge you four bills per pill. Nice racket if you can create it. Other drugs they get are more interesting and far more regulated. Opioid medicines, for instance, required someone to account for them at each step of their journey. Despite this, they ended up stolen and distributed illegally with alarming frequency.

I wondered if the withdrawals from his savings were payments to delivery people or suppliers. *Here's some cash to look the other way while I grab this box.* Then the contents of said box could be sold, generating funds for the deposits I saw. The amount of money meant it would need to be more than an occasional box. I knew some rich people who could have lived nicely on George's money.

Rich needed to know this. It was another path to

the investigation. We could drive to West Virginia and nose around. Rich would complain about jurisdiction, but he was already out of his, and I was only licensed to investigate within the state of Maryland, so we needed to confine the out-of-state investigative task force to the two of us. I shut everything down and walked next door to Rich's room.

I wished I possessed more information.

* * *

"I WANT to bring in the FBI," Rich said when I brain-dumped everything to him.

I hadn't expected him to want to run to the feds. There were jurisdiction concerns, and there was punting to the goddamn FBI when it wasn't even fourth down. On top of it all, I didn't want to tell them how I got my information or even what information I gathered on George Russell. "You've certainly proposed a solution," I said.

"You don't agree?"

"Of course not."

"Let me guess," he said. "You don't want to share your info with the feds."

"I don't even want them to know I *have* info," I said. "If it's all the same, I'd prefer to keep my intelligence-gathering methods out of this. They're going to have too many questions."

"I think this is getting bigger than you and me."

"How? So far, we know Land of the Brave looks shady. We know the boss has a brother who might be making money buying and selling pills out of his hospital. This isn't a drug cartel in action here."

Rich crossed his arms under his chest. "You want to risk the investigation because of your shady methods," he said, shaking his head. "Incredible."

"What's the risk to the investigation?" I said. "You and I can do this."

"I think there are more people involved than a charity director and a hospital boss."

"Sure. They have to have a driver or two somewhere, plus the four assholes we sent to the hospital. If those are the best goons they can muster up, I'm not worried."

"This is about Jim!" Rich's face grew red. "I want justice for Jim, justice for his family, justice for—"

"Yourself?"

Rich sighed and glared at me. "I was going to say his kids, but I'm his friend, so yes, for myself, too."

"I don't think we should bring in the feds," I said. "We can do this."

"We have people in Maryland and West Virginia involved," said Rich. "We're talking interstate crime."

"Great. You bring in the feds. When they take over everything, lock you out, and bungle it, don't say I didn't warn you. Even if they don't fuck it up, you're looking at months to get your justice. Hope you have a lot of vacation days." I turned toward the door.

"Where are you going?"

"Back to Baltimore," I said. "You bring in the FBI, I'm out."

"How are you going to get there?" Rich said.

"I'll take an Uber." I grabbed the knob and pulled the door open.

"Wait."

I stopped.

"I still think this is bigger than the two of us."

"Have fun getting stonewalled by the FBI, then," I said.

"If I don't call them, what would your next steps be?"

"I want to look into the brother and his hospital."

"And if we build a case against him?"

"Then we close it," I said, turning back to face Rich. "You came out here to get justice for your friend. If you want to farm it out to someone else, whatever. Up to you, but you're not getting justice then. Someone else is."

"I don't see it the same way," said Rich.

"You and I often see these things differently."

Rich uncrossed and crossed his arms again. He pursed his lips, rolled his eyes, shook his head. If steam poured out his ears, I would consider my triumph complete. "Thanks to you," he said, "I'm not convinced we can trust the locals."

"Agreed."

"Fine. We'll keep it small for now. If this gets too big for us, though, I'm going to call in some help."

"Not the feds?" I said.

"State Police," Rich said. "I know a guy. He's trustworthy. We can work with him."

"Who decides if the case overwhelms us?"

"I do. My judgment. If you don't like it, go call your fucking Uber."

I grinned. "Really, Rich?"

"What?"

"You don't *call* an Uber. You use the app."

Rich chuckled and dropped his arms. "Go back to your room," he said.

So I did.

* * *

MY FATHER's deep exhalation over the phone made a sibilant hiss in my ear. "I'm not sure this is what we envisioned when we set this up, son," he said.

When I left Hong Kong after thirty-nine months, it was with the strong encouragement of the Chinese government. They arrested my hacker friends and me and threw a bunch of charges at us, but the ones they cared about the most were helping Americans and dissidents hide from the government or leave the country. Most of those things fell on me. My compatriots were into embarrassing the communists, going after their banks, and similar things. I did some of it, too, but even then, my conscience reared its ugly head and compelled me to help people.

After returning to the States, my parents threatened to cut me off from the family fortune unless I got a job helping people. Seeing as I'd burned through most of my money in China, I was forced to consider their position. Before long, I settled on being a private investigator, and got my license thanks to some embellishment of the legitimacy of my work in China. The kicker was I wouldn't charge my clients. My parents hired me into their foundation and would pay me for solving cases. So far, this arrangement chafed me but worked reasonably well. Until this case, apparently.

"What do you mean, Dad?"

"Rich wasn't who we had in mind for your clients."

"I told you the details of the case," I said. "You don't think the family sounds like they need help?"

"I guess so," he said. "It's merely. . . irregular, is all. Clients usually come to you."

"Rich did."

"You know what I mean."

"Do you think it was easy for him, Dad? You know how Rich and I have gotten along—or not—over the years. Since I started this job, he's taken every chance he could to run down the way I do things."

"You never thought his points were perhaps valid?" said my father.

"I'm sure they have some merit," I said, "but Rich and I are very different people. He has trouble with anyone who doesn't do things by the book."

"What are you getting at, son?"

"My point is it took a lot for Rich to approach me for help. He needed to swallow his pride and choke down a bunch of objections about my methods. I could have given him shit for coming to me, but I recognized what it took for him to do it. Maybe you should, too."

Silence was my only reply for a few seconds. Then my father said, "All right. I think you've got a valid point as well. We'll be interested to hear how this one turns out."

"So will I," I said.

"Should your mother start looking for western Maryland newspapers?"

"Dad, I'm not sure the two of you could be seen reading a paper called the *Republican*. What would your rich liberal friends think?"

"I'll let your mother worry about it," he said. We both knew she would. It was probably the thing she did best in the world. OK, maybe tied with sniffing and tsking after I offended her sensibilities. "What are you going to do next?"

"I think we're going to poke around the organization," I said. "They're our best lead right now. Maybe our only lead."

"Good luck, son. You're a long way from Baltimore."

I looked at my motel room. It didn't offer a view of Route 219, but the images had been seared into my head the last couple days. "Don't I know it," I said.

CHAPTER 7

Fairmont Regional Medical Center ran a slick-looking website. No doubt it had been designed by a well-coiffed chap (or chapette) who sat in the dark and sipped lattes while writing the code. It wasn't built on WordPress or Wix or any other do-it-yourself platform. Whoever created it made a professional, functional, and mostly clean website. The architect even required secure connections over the web.

None of this stopped me from hitting it with a scanner. Services run on ports, many of which are assigned specific numbers, and the scanning program tells me which ones are running. It didn't take long to find the weak link. An older version of File Transfer Protocol was still used for exactly what its name suggests. The problem: it was designed in the infancy of the Internet. No one thought about security then. Thus, no security was ever built into FTP. Everything it transmitted, including login credentials and the contents of files, got sent over the wire in the clear. Unencrypted.

Because FTP is an older protocol, the versions of it

installed on web servers are frequently outdated. In other cases, the protocol will accept default login credentials because whoever configured the server never bothered to remove them. The FTP version was current, so I looked up this particular implementation's default credentials. I tried them.

They worked.

Sometimes, it really does prove so easy. While I like to think I'm good at the advanced hacking stuff, there are occasions when simple tactics are the home run hitters. The login I used provided full access to the file system. FTP uses simple commands to list directories and upload and download files. I spent a few minutes nosing around and seeing what directories could house juicy information. My searching turned up a scad of interesting documents, including a listing of privileged accounts. I downloaded them all to my laptop and disconnected all my sessions.

Combing through data was not exciting. I contemplated walking outside and watching some grass grow for a change of pace because of time to kill while Rich went to Jim's funeral. When he mentioned it, I didn't offer to go. He wouldn't want me there. Rich needed his space in a time like this; I understood and respected it. Besides, it gave me the chance to conduct a riveting review of hospital files.

About ninety minutes later, I finished reading all the pilfered material. Nothing jumped out at me as irregular. I even logged back in with an admin account I found on the list, downloaded more documents, and read those. The hospital maintained impeccable logs of all drugs in and out, and they meticulously dotted each I and crossed every T in triplicate when it came to controlled substances. Boxes of Vicodin weren't getting up and walking out the door.

How else could George bring drugs in? I looked for shipments of opioids delivered to the wrong locations, stolen from another facility, or hijacked in transit. The number of results probably shouldn't have surprised me, but it did. A package arriving at the wrong destination could happen. There is no malice in human error. The others, though, involved both malice and muscle. I thought of the four goons who darkened our doorsteps. Give them ski masks and guns, and they could probably abscond with a bunch of stolen drugs.

A box of fentanyl going missing from LA didn't mean much, however. I narrowed my focus. If George Russell sent people to steal drugs, those thefts needed to happen within driving distance of his hospital. You couldn't sneak a bunch of controlled medication on a commercial flight, and using a chartered plane would add both expense and another person who could talk. No, George's crew would stay fairly local. Being a professional detective, I employed the advanced sleuthing tactic of making up a number and setting a search radius of two hundred fifty miles.

Sure enough, I found some. A report of an irregular delivery to Fairmont Regional. A delivery of opioids knocked over outside Pittsburgh three years ago. Another near Charleston, West Virginia, six months after. Yet another near Winchester, Virginia, five months later. I expanded the search radius and found them going back a couple more years, always every five to six months, never more than three in a calendar year. Local cops and the feds were investigating, of course. I read up on the robberies. Different vehicles used every time. Never the same physical descriptions of the crew.

Different clothes, masks, and guns each time. No one killed, though a few guards took beatings here and there.

While I read over everything, Rich returned from the funeral. I heard the rumble of the Camaro's V8 in the parking lot, like the low growl of a wild animal. A minute later, he knocked on the door. "It's Rich." I knew already, both from the Camaro and his knock. Rich, despite being a little shorter than me, has larger hands, and the way he bangs on a door is distinct. Kind of like clubbing a tree with a hammer.

I let him in. We chatted about the funeral for a minute before getting down to new business. I told him what I'd discovered about George Russell, his hospital, and the pattern of stolen opioids. "Fuck," Rich said. I found this an adequate summary. "What do you think they're doing with the drugs?"

"Selling them," I said. "My guess is George's random deposits equate to his share of the proceeds."

"Of course they're selling them, but what's the method? How do you move a pile of stolen pills?"

" Not only move them, but do it regularly. They restock a couple times a year."

Rich shook his head. He tried to run a hand through his hair, but his crew cut made the gesture look ridiculous. "I know the manufacturers have tons of pills," he said. "It's a shame . . . they probably didn't even notice the missing stock."

I was about to point out our focus needed to be on distribution when Rich's phone buzzed. He looked it at, frowned, and put it away. "Connie just texted," he said. "Land of the Brave is picking up Jim's last batch of honey tomorrow morning."

Neither of us said anything for a minute. Then the

light bulb went on for me. It must have gone on for Rich, too, because his eyes went wide, and his mouth fell open. "The pickups," I said. "They pick up whatever legit products the veterans have, add their drugs, and distribute them through middle men."

Rich's mouth clicked shut. He nodded. "Makes sense. You said the robbery crews seemed to change a lot?"

"Yes."

"I wonder if some of the people giving product to the pickup guy were giving more than honey and vegetables."

I thought about it for a moment. "Rich," I said, "you know what this could mean."

"No," he said. "Jim wouldn't take part in something like this."

"I don't think we can be sure of—"

"I can be sure of it!"

We couldn't get anywhere this way. Rich would get pissed and tell me to call an Uber again. I had no proof, anyway, so I dropped it. For now. "Fine. But I think you know what we need to do next."

"I do."

"How are your following skills?"

"Good enough to make up for having a big blue Camaro," said Rich.

* * *

EARLY THE NEXT MORNING, Rich and I sat in his car. He parked three houses away from the Sheltons'. We each held the largest coffee Sheetz sold, which was twenty-four ounces. I could have used half again as many. I ate a turkey sausage breakfast burrito of above-average flavor. Rich scarfed down a couple donuts and a bearclaw pastry the size of an actual ursine paw. I couldn't believe he still ate such garbage. Rich is about six and a half years older than me, making him thirty-six. Not yet twenty-nine, I possessed the metabolism to shrug off a morning of ingesting sugary rubbish. Rich was at an age where he could pay for such indulgences. Of course, he had been six feet tall and a solid two hundred pounds for so long, I wondered if he skipped birth and came into the world fully formed.

"How do you think this all went down?" he said after chomping a chunk of the pastry.

I considered making a crack about Rich's breakfast but refrained. Doing pastry puns before eight is not in my wheelhouse. "I think George found out where shipments were going," I said. "He could have access to the information. Then he would tell Pete, who would rustle up a crew."

"I hate this case," Rich said. "Jim Shelton dies, and a bunch of other veterans were probably used as robbers."

"Maybe they got paid in drugs," I said. "Some of them already could have issues."

"It's possible." Rich's nostrils flared. His knuckles were white as he gripped the steering wheel. If we got to arrest Pete and George, they would need some of their own pilfered painkillers after Rich finished with them.

"We'll get them," I said.

"I know . . . and I want to make sure we do it as right as possible."

We differed on methodology. If I found a corner to cut, I would. Technology was a wonderful thing. Rich, by contrast, would quote chapter and verse from the law and the police manual. Our styles didn't mesh. Despite this, we ended up working together in some capacity on most of my cases. I was still surprised Rich wanted me to come with him out here. He knew enough friends on the force to invite someone with a similar level of love for the rulebooks.

Silence ruled the day for the next few minutes. I finished my breakfast burrito, and Rich washed down the last of his pastry with a big swig of coffee. We watched the Shelton house. Nothing. The clock ticked eight. The pickup driver was now officially late. None of the other houses showed any activity. It was a sleepy Saturday morning for everyone except us. I witnessed several leaves shake free of trees in the wind and spiral to the ground. The last of my coffee went down my throat. It was good. I wished they sold a bigger cup.

At about ten after, a cargo van pulled up in front of the Sheltons' house. It was white, no windows after the passenger compartment, and no lettering on the side. Perfectly nondescript. Even if someone saw this vehicle involved in something illicit, there were hundreds like it on the roads at any given time. I wondered if it was stolen. I figured the plates were, or a set would be if the driver or his boss sniffed anything suspicious. A man got out and walked toward the house. His back to us, he looked short and dumpy. If someone stole merchandise from him, he wasn't catching the thief on foot.

The driver knocked on the door. From my angle, I couldn't see anything happening inside. He left the porch a minute later and walked around to the back. I saw Connie Shelton in the backyard. She directed him to the shed, which she unlocked. The driver picked up three boxes. Each was about the size of those paper ream boxes from office supply stores. Connie locked the shed, and the driver carried his haul to the van. Rich and I both slumped down in our seats. He went to the rear of the vehicle, and a moment later, climbed back in behind the wheel. We stayed low while he turned around and drove down the street the way he came.

Rich fired up the Camaro, and it roared to life like a lion denied his breakfast. He eased it onto the roads. We kept the van in our sights. With no rear windows, the driver needed his exterior mirrors to see anything behind him. I figured this would help us follow him, but Rich was the expert here. We got onto Route 219 and took it out of the city onto Route 39. It wound around a lot and became Route 7 after we crossed the West Virginia border. Other twisty-turny roads followed, and I stopped keeping track of the numbers. The Camaro hugged the curves, allowing Rich to keep a reasonable distance behind the van. An old pickup truck got between us at some point.

We soon got onto I-79. Ten miles later, we were back on West Virginia county roads. I expected to hear someone whistle "Dixie" every time we drove past a farmhouse. Eventually, we left Route 19 for Village Way. A large brick building loomed ahead, most likely our destination. The van turned into the delivery entrance. Rich eased the Camaro into a parking lot on the other side of the street, affording us a good view of all the comings and goings. We waited.

Outside Fairmont Regional Medical Center.

* * *

"WHAT DO you think he's doing in there?" I said.

"Probably picking up drugs," said Rich.

"Pretty brazen to distribute them right from the hospital."

"It's also pretty brazen to rob opioid shipments."

This was certainly true. The whole operation was bold. I hated referring to it this way because it sounded like a compliment, and I didn't want to offer praise to the kind of assholes who got people hooked on drugs and murdered veterans. "So if he's adding drugs to those boxes," I said, "we should see where he takes them."

"I plan to," Rich said.

"And then what?"

"We lean on somebody."

"Who?" I said.

"Depends," he said. "Maybe the driver, if he seems like he'll knuckle under. Or maybe whoever he drops the drugs off to."

"He could be making more than one stop."

Rich nodded. "True. This network could be bigger than we thought."

It must have been. I thought the problem lay in Oakland at first. It showed all the signs, but cities across the border in West Virginia were in similar straits. Jobs drying up affected people in both states. Vicodin, oxycodone, and similar pills filled some gaps for people who had holes in the center of them. Eventually, the drugs ruled their lives. Sometimes, they ended their lives. Mostly, they ruined them. This was a nationwide problem. We were seeing it in two communities. We could shut Land of the Brave down, but doing so wouldn't get rid of everyone's pills or addictions. Other suppliers would fill the vacuum. I didn't know how to stop the problem here, and I didn't envy anyone who tried to reverse it on a larger scale.

A few minutes later, we saw the van emerge from the delivery entrance. Rich left the parking lot and pulled out behind him. As we drove, I felt the weight of the .45 holstered at my left side. The chase was on again. I wondered where it would take us.

CHAPTER 8

THE FIRST STOP WAS ABOUT TEN MINUTES AWAY. The van pulled into the parking lot of a small grocery store. Rich drove past and parked at a Chinese restaurant about a hundred yards away. The driver carried one box inside. It was a different guy this time, taller and much slimmer. "New driver," I said. Rich didn't answer. "I guess the boxes still have honey in them."

"Maybe."

"I know they're running a brazen operation, but it would be another level entirely to deliver nothing but drugs to a market."

"I guess," Rich said. He narrowed his eyes and looked around. The grocery store was part of a small strip mall. A third of the businesses were shuttered. Some of their names were still visible as the cleaner portions of the stone front the letters occupied stood out against the grime. I counted five boarded-up windows and doors. You could see more driving down several streets in Baltimore. "Too many people." Rich kept looking around. "His stop doesn't look too busy, but some of the other places are. We can't accost this asshole here."

I nodded. "I guess we'll have to see where he goes next."

"If he takes one box to each stop, he should have two more."

"And the farther he gets from the hospital, maybe the farther he gets from anyone who would help him."

Rich grinned. "There are occasions I like the way you think," he said.

"Try it more often," I said. "You might come to love it."

"No, thanks."

"It doesn't suit you," I said.

"What's that supposed to mean?"

"You are who you are, Rich. You're a guy who knows and respects the law. You've done well for yourself. I'm honestly shocked you're even out of your jurisdiction with your scofflaw cousin."

"I could have brought some cops," Rich said.

"I'm surprised you didn't."

Rich took a deep breath. He did it a lot when he was deep in thought. "You're right; your way of thinking doesn't suit me. It suits you. Another cop would probably think too much like me. Even someone like Paul King." He was another BPD detective. He played faster and looser than Rich, especially in areas of personal grooming, but when it came down to it, King was a cop. Serve and protect. Uphold the law. I came from a different world where rules and statutes often got in the way. The world was flexible, and the law wasn't. People like Rich didn't see this as a problem. People like me bent the law to find solutions.

"If I didn't know better," I said, "I would think you paid me a compliment there."

"Good thing you know better," Rich said with a grin.

The driver walked out of the store, sans box, and got back into his van. He pulled onto the main road. We were close behind him. Rich followed well. He drove a distinctive car, which was a negative, but he always kept a reasonable distance, drove in other lanes, and didn't care if another car came between him and the target. The dickhead in the van hadn't given any indication he was wise to a tail. Of course, if four more dickheads got out of a crew cab pickup at the next stop, we'd know he spotted us. So far, so good.

"So many overdoses out here," Rich said.

I had done a little reading. Certain parts of West Virginia were especially hard-hit by the opioid crisis. Children as young as twelve overdosed and died. Elderly folks in their eighties met the same fate. People tended to think of drug addiction as some kind of failing of a person's character or moral fiber. The problem there is no twelve-year-old ODs because of character defects. This was a medical problem, and I was encouraged by signs of progress in treating it as such. A documentary about opioids in the area even won an Oscar.

Even with all those factors, it surprised me Rich was wise to the problem. His computer probably had more cobwebs than gigs of RAM. "I'm impressed," I said.

"You're not the only one who can use Google," said Rich.

We settled in behind the van. Thirty minutes and no sign of a stop. We took a road or two I was surprised had ever been paved. Rich hung back father on the less-traveled ones. About fifteen minutes later, we approached a small, nondescript town. The van made a left and then pulled into an alley behind a building serving as a combination clinic and veterinarian. *Get your dog's nails clipped while you wait for your flu shot!* I hoped they were more clever in their advertising.

Rich idled the Camaro on the street. We could barely see the van around the corner of the building. The driver got out, took the remaining two boxes out of the back, and disappeared. "How many clinics you know use honey?" said Rich.

I shrugged. "Could be some holistic quack in there," I said.

"How many of them you think set up shop in small-town West Virginia?"

"Maybe there's a demand for honey on the vet side of the business."

Rich snorted. "I think they're more likely delivering straight drugs here," he said.

"I doubt it," I said. "Keeping them in the boxes with honey is important. What if this shithead gets pulled over and a deputy wants to look in the back. 'See, just boxes of honey.' Lots easier to explain than a box crammed full of pills."

"I guess." Rich pulled forward. "Alley looks empty." It was and ran more than the length of the building, but other than a Dumpster, the white van was the only thing there. "This is his last stop. We'll need to talk to this asshole here." Rich squeezed past the van and parked the Camaro on the other side of the Dumpster. We got out and walked toward the clinic's rear entrance. I stood on one side, and Rich took the other.

We waited.

* * *

MUTED CONVERSATIONS and chuckles made their way through the heavy back door. In my youth, my friends and I would shout at each other under water in a pool. The water, of course, distorted our voices to inarticulate screams. The voices coming from the clinic reminded me of those days. I fidgeted. Patience could not be counted first among my virtues. I looked around the alley. Trash lined the walls, increasing in volume nearer the Dumpster. I also saw two broken hypodermic needles and wondered how much more drug paraphernalia blended in too well with the detritus to be obvious.

Rich stared at the door. His right hand waited to grab his gun; his left curled into a fist. In the quiet of the alley, I could hear his measured breathing. In, out. Even. Between Afghanistan and Baltimore, I wondered how many dangerous scenarios Rich willingly walked into. By now, his slow breathing became automatic in situations like this. I didn't have any routines. I simply wandered into danger and figured I would come out okay on the other side. So far, so good.

The voices inside fell silent. Footsteps replaced them, moving closer. The door arced open, toward me, blocking my view. I couldn't see the driver. I heard him start to say something, but then Rich clamped a hand over his mouth and shoved him into the wall. The door clicked shut. The driver's eyes threatened to bulge from his head as they flittered between Rich and me. "Stay quiet," Rich said through clenched teeth. "You make a lot of noise . . . it won't go well for you. Understand?" The driver nodded. "We want information. Let's start with your name." Rich took his hand away and balled it into a fist. This did not escape the other man's notice.

"Billy," he said in a small voice. Billy might have been in his mid-twenties, but he spent those years doing some hard living. I figured he'd been sampling the delivery product, maybe even taking part of his pay in something like Vicodin. He stood a hair shorter than Rich, but would only weigh 140 pounds if he'd just gone swimming in his clothes. The color of his skin would encourage a mortician to embalm him. His clothes were at least a size too big. When he talked, I could tell he needed to spend about a week in a dentist's chair.

"Billy, I see you're making some deliveries," said Rich.

"Who are you?" Billy said. Rich showed him his badge. "You ain't even in the right state. Shit, man." Confidence brightened Billy's dull eyes. "I ain't gotta talk to you." He pushed off the wall.

Billy hit the wall again right away when Rich punched him in the face. He took the off-the-clock proviso seriously. I never saw him cuff someone around under these circumstances in Baltimore. Billy shook off the cobwebs and grimaced. "What the hell?" he said.

"I told you," said Rich, "we have some questions. You don't get to walk away until we're done."

After more looking between Rich and me, Billy accepted his fate and hung his head. "What do you want to know."

"Everything," I said. "Let's start with collection and delivery."

"OK. We pick up stuff from people who work on the land."

"How often?"

Billy shrugged. "Once a week, usually. Sometimes more often in summer. There's more to pick up then."

Growing seasons were not a mystery to me, but I nodded as if Billy said something profound. It seemed to placate him. Then Rich said, "How many guys make the pickups?"

"Five or six."

"They all look like you?"

"What are you trying to say?"

"I think you know, you skinny prick," Rich said. He crowded Billy, who shrank back into the wall.

"No, no," he said. "Some of them are bigger."

"Like four guys who could play offensive line?" I said.

"Yeah." Billy nodded. "Them, me, sometimes another guy."

"Then what do you do?"

"We take the shit somewhere," Billy said. "Usually the hospital. Sometimes back to base."

"'Base' being Land of the Brave?" Rich said.

"Yeah. Depends where the deliveries are."

"Then you add drugs to whatever you collected," I said.

"We have a guy at each place who does that," Billy said. "They know how to pack everything. If we get stopped, the cops only see honey or vegetables or whatever."

"What if they look closer?" Rich said.

"Then they'd find the pills. Shit ain't invisible. But you ain't gonna see it unless you go looking for it."

"OK, you make deliveries," I said. "Places like this, grocery stores, whatever. Then they sell the pills."

"Yeah," Billy said as if I'd asked him a super obvious

questions. And I did, but we needed to confirm the basics.

"Then what happens with the money, asshole? Do you and the no-neck quartet go back and collect it?"

"No. Unless we need to. Then those other four guys go out. Usually, the places just pay. I'm not sure how it works. They don't tell me shit like that.

For good reason, I thought, but I said, "OK, Billy. Maybe a few more questions."

Before I could ask another one, Rich broke in. "How many places do you deliver to?"

"I usually get the same spots," Billy said. "Different days. I guess about ten in all."

"All in West Virginia?" he nodded. "Your collections, too?" Another nod. "You never go to Maryland?" Head shake.

"Wait a minute," I said. "Do any guys in Maryland cross over into West Virginia?"

"Nope. We all stay in our states."

"No interstate commerce." Rich frowned when I spoke those words. "Smart."

"Let's give an award to the criminals," Rich grumbled.

"Am I done?" Billy asked.

"No," Rich and I said at the same time.

I didn't think of anything else we needed him for. Billy was a pickup and delivery guy. He knew exactly what he needed to know to do those jobs. The Russell brothers controlled the information and managed the schedules and routes. They did illegal things, but their drivers never crossed state lines and only made collections when they needed to strong-arm someone. I'm sure a federal lawyer could pin something big on them, but Land of the Brave skirted initial scrutiny. Exactly like their deliveries.

"What else you need?" Billy said. "I told you what I know."

Rich looked at me. I shrugged. "I think we're done," Rich said. Billy started to walk away, but Rich shoved him back into the wall. "Listen, Billy. You're not going to tell anyone about our little chat."

"No?" A spark of defiance lit in Billy's eyes. "Why not?"

"One of my friends died because of the assholes you work for. I have no problem evening the score." Billy stared at Rich, and his expression morphed into one of fear.

"Sure," he said. "You got it. Not a word."

"You'd better be telling the truth." Rich let Billy go. He dashed back to his van like someone fired him out of a sling. With screeching tires, he pulled away.

"Think he's going to dime us out?" I said.

"I doubt it," Rich said. "He looked terrified I was going to kill him."

"If I didn't know you better, I would have thought you'd shoot him on the spot."

"It was tempting." Rich took a deep breath. "Pieces of shit like him got Jim Shelton killed."

"And we'll pin it on them," I said. "All of them. But we'll do it the right way."

"The right way?" Rich said with a smirk. "You?"

"OK," I said, "some allowances need to be made."

CHAPTER 9

WE DROVE AWAY FROM THE CLINIC AFTER I convinced Rich not to kick the front door in and raid the place. He wanted to call the West Virginia police. This was another ledge I talked him off. Short-term satisfaction didn't help us bust Land of the Brave and everyone involved. If the clinic folks got hauled away, the Russell brothers might pack their bags and set up shop in parts unknown. It took a couple minutes, but Rich listened to reason. I wondered what the hell happened to make me the sensible one.

Back at the motel, Rich went to his room, and I returned to mine. He said he wanted to strategize. It worked for me, because I needed to exercise. Too much sitting in the motel, driving around, and eating fast food left me feeling a little sluggish. I changed into a running outfit and pounded the pavement on Route 219. Federal Hill certainly offered more scenic routes, but miles were miles. While I ran, I thought about Billy. Rich definitely scared him, but his four large friends knew where we stayed. He could rat us out, and they could come back, this time with a bunch of guns. I wondered if we should switch to a different place even though we weren't swamped with options.

After four miles, I walked back into my room and took a shower. Once dressed, I knocked on Rich's door to ask if he wanted food. We decided on subs from Sheetz. At this point, Rich and I should have owned stock in the company after our many visits. If being a shareholder got me free coffee, I would take it. I got two subs, a couple bags of chips, some peanuts, and a pair of drinks. I carried it all back to the motel.

As I approached, I noticed the large SUV near our rooms again. "Shit," I muttered as I ducked behind a pickup truck. Rich's door was ajar. My gun was in my room. I was armed with a pocket knife and a bag of food against who knew how many armed goons in the room. Not good. I couldn't wade into those odds.

A minute later, three of the four men we saw before led Rich out of his room, each of them with a pistol trained on him. Two shoved him into the back of the SUV, while the third kicked my door in. A few seconds later, he emerged, shaking his head. He got into the SUV, and it drove off. I scurried into a better hiding spot behind the truck. The SUV made a left onto 219.

I ran back into my room and grabbed my pistol. The one who searched merely looked around; had he opened the nightstand drawer, he would have taken my .45. I stuffed it into the back of my jeans and dashed into Rich's room. His car keys were hidden behind the TV, where he always leaves them. I picked them up, ran out of the room, and fired up the Camaro. Rich likes to practice what he calls "tactical parking," so he backed into his parking spot. This allowed me to mash my foot to the floor and screech out in a trail of smoke.

Without stopping, I made the left onto 219. One

car coming from my left slowed, and I fit the Camaro in front of someone coming from the right. The SUV had already turned off the road. I figured they were going the way Rich and I went a couple nights ago, so I made the right turn and got back on the gas. The Camaro was a big, heavy beast, and visibility in any direction was subpar. But its fantastic American-made V8 knew what to do when I pressed the accelerator. The car surged ahead, and I scanned every cross street for the SUV.

Then I saw it through the trees around a bend ahead. I backed off the throttle and kept the other vehicle in sight without riding up on them. They probably knew Rich's car, and while I had no idea how observant these assholes were, I didn't want them seeing a blue Camaro in the rearview mirror. I kept my distance as we drove on, farther than Rich and I went. Ahead, they made a left turn onto a street full of ramshackle houses. I slowed, approached the intersection, and watched. This was a short street with three houses on each side. None of them looked fit for human residence. The SUV stopped in front of the last one on the left.

I backed up and pulled over. Through the trees lining the street, I saw the three men lead Rich into the house. The door closed, and I saw the X. I eased my way onto the street, parking behind a huge truck in front of the first house on the left. There were only two other non-goon vehicles. They looked as bad as the homes. I wondered if anyone still lived on this street. A couple lights went on inside the last house. I got out of the Camaro and closed the door as gently as I could. The street was quiet enough I could hear my own steps as I approached. I crouched behind a rusted old SUV parked at the edge of the house. The late afternoon sun wouldn't hide me. Everything was silent.

What would Rich do in this situation? Probably call for backup. I didn't have any readily available. The county police were still dodgy to me, and I didn't want to bring them in. The state police were farther away. Anyone else I could call would need a few hours to arrive. I was on my own. A couple months ago, I donned a helmet and bulletproof vest and raided a building with Rich and some other cops. This was a different situation altogether. I had a pistol, no extra ammo, no protection, and no backup. If I went in, I had to do it strategically. If they saw me, Rich could die.

A couple minutes later, two of the men walked out of the house and got in the front seats of their vehicle. I wondered where the other one was. The two in the SUV didn't look in a hurry to leave. I pondered the survivability of making a dash for the door when the other one sprinted out of the building. I sneaked around to the far side of the truck. Once the third asshole got inside, they took off. I could see them laughing. Cold welled in the pit of my stomach as I wondered what they could find so funny.

When I looked back at the house, I saw.

It was on fire.

* * *

FLAMES PEEKED from windows at the back of the house. I could see bright orange through what remained of the glass. Black clouds wafted out, also at the back. They must have started the blaze there. I ran, sucked in a breath, and pushed the front door open. Acrid smoke greeted me, pouring forth and stinging my eyes. I pulled my shirt over my nose and mouth. The kitchen was an inferno, and the flames spread out from there. Much of the first floor was already ablaze. I saw a sea of gray broken up by pockets of brilliant orange. "Rich!" I shouted. No response. I coughed amid the smoke. "Rich!"

"Up here," I heard him say.

I stayed low and moved in the direction of his voice. As I got closer, I could see the outline of a staircase. A couple steps were missing, and what remained looked like it would collapse under a featherweight boxer. If I went bounding up them, I would wind up on the floor. And while I felt sure I could scramble from the house before it became a pile of cinders, Rich may not make it to safety. I couldn't take the chance. "Are you all right?" I said.

"They tied me up," he called.

"I'm coming up." I put a foot on the bottom step. It didn't buckle. One down. A dozen or so to go.

The second stair held my weight, too. The third was missing. I stepped onto the fourth. It squeaked but didn't give. When I pushed off the second and put all my weight on the fourth step, it wobbled. I hopped to the fifth. The sixth and seventh were fine, but the eighth was gone. I did the same thing I'd done to bypass the third. The ninth held. The tenth buckled. When my foot hit the eleventh, the step broke. Wood clawed at my ankle as I clutched the railing, which was barely in better shape than the staircase.

The splintered edges cut my skin. I felt warm blood run into my sock. The railing threatened to pull away from the wall. It took a few seconds, but I extracted my lower leg and made it the rest of the way up. I spared a glance behind me. The all-consuming gray engulfed the lower level. Going back down would not be an option. My chest and throat burned.

I crouched in a hallway in the middle of the second floor. Smoke filtered up here through the vents and the holes in the floor. Heat radiated from the bottom floor. I was already covered in sweat. I coughed a few times. The air was better up here but getting worse as the fire raged below. It wouldn't take much to burn the shambles of this level. Holes were missing from the walls and ceiling. Water damage pockmarked many of the remaining surfaces. I could make out at least two doors looking at me in both directions.

"Where are you?" I said.

"Here." To my right.

I wanted to run along the hall but was concerned the floor would crumble beneath me. Jogging while staying as low as I could would have to suffice. I found Rich in the remains of a bedroom. An old mattress lay in tatters against the wall. The rest of the room looked as bad as the rest of the house and smelled worse. The arsonists left Rich tied to metal chair. He was bound at the wrists and around the ankles. I took out my pocket knife and spent a minute cutting him free.

"Thanks," he said. "How'd you know I was here?"

"I was coming back when they were loading you into the SUV. Let's talk later. This shithole is coming down."

Rich grabbed his gun off the floor in what once was a closet. He put it in the back of his jeans. "Stairs?" he said.

"Total loss," I said. "The first floor is an inferno by now." Sweat threatened to run into my eyes, which already stung. This end of the house was better for now. If we stood here much longer, though, smoke would overcome us. It already flowed from the vent.

Rich looked at the window. The glass had long since broken and fallen away, some of it into the room. He shoved the frame open. "We can get out here." He pointed down. "Look. It must be a carport or a shed." A roof jutted from the rest of the house's first level. We could make the short drop to there and then either climb or jump down.

"You go first," I said. "Your car is waiting outside."

Rich climbed through the window and stood on the ledge, facing away from me. He made the short leap to the roof. I heard a crack and saw a few shingles scatter when he landed, but the carport—or whatever it was— remained intact. Rich moved to the edge, grabbed on, swung his legs over, and dropped to the ground. I saw him look around. "Shit. I think they're back. A gray SUV pulled up. Must want to check out their handiwork."

"They will have seen your car on the way in," I said. "They know I'm here, too."

Rich drew his gun. "Then get down here, and let's deal with them." He crouched and skulked away toward the other end of the house.

I eased over the windowsill and onto the narrow ledge. It was about three, maybe four feet down to the roof. I jumped and landed atop the carport. It made another crack, louder than the first. Before I could take a step, the roof buckled and caved in, and I went down with it. I'd felt it start to go, and the realization gave me enough time to protect my head in the fall. The rest of me hit the concrete floor of the carport hard. I lay there, surrounded by a few planks and beams. I coughed, and my whole body hurt. If this were a normal fall, I could have sprung back to my feet, even in pain. The fire sapped my strength, though. I wanted to lie on the floor, but I knew I didn't have the luxury. Rich would need help.

While I summoned the energy to stand, the rest of the roof above me groaned. It shimmed, shook, and then fell on me.

CHAPTER 10

I never lost consciousness. As with the fall, I had just enough time to protect my head. The roof battering me doubled the pain I was already in. I might have welcomed the anesthetics of a blow to the noggin, but if the goon squad got past Rich, I'd be easy pickings lying knocked out amid a pile of old wood. If I wanted to be any help to Rich—and myself—I needed to get out of here. The light lumber landing on my arms when I covered my head fell away easily enough.

Next, the three planks lying on my chest. They flew off with a shove which sent a flare of pain blazing down my shoulder. My legs were pinned by a beam across my thighs and a bunch of two-by-fours below my knees. The larger piece of wood did not respond to my first push. I shifted my hips as much as I could, put both arms under the beam, and heaved. It lifted about a foot. My left arm screamed at me. I didn't have the strength or pain tolerance to throw it off. Instead, I turned more and thrust my arms upward. The beam crashed back to the concrete about two inches above my head. I let out a deep breath.

Behind me, the fire raged. A window somewhere in the house popped and sprayed glass into the backyard. I heard voices. Before I crashed through the carport's roof, Rich left to hunt for the men who brought him here. I needed to help him. They numbered three when they kidnapped him and could have picked up the fourth. I sat up. My left shoulder still hurt something fierce, and the rest of my body was one large dull ache. I reached behind me for my gun.

It wasn't there.

I heard voices again. Harsh, unfamiliar. Definitely not Rich. I looked around for the .45 but didn't see it. It must have fallen out when I took my tumble and got buried by the roof. I rummaged through the detritus. Most of it was brown and darkened by water damage. The color made finding a black gun difficult. If I survived this, maybe I could bling out my arsenal with some nickel grips.

A shot cracked, then wood splintered. I searched faster. Three more blasts came from the direction of the splintering. I heard what sounded like two people grunting and falling over. Digging through a pile, my hand bumped something metal. The gun. I grabbed it, then crouched and looked out from behind a pile of wood in the ruins of the carport. One of the goons ran from my left. Out of the corner of my eye, I saw Rich coming from the right. He stayed close to the house and used the shadows of trees as he moved. The other man didn't see him. By the time he did, Rich was ten feet away, and the shot was easy.

Rich looked at the wreckage and frowned. "You all right?"

"I'll live," I said.

"Stay here. I'm pretty sure they brought a fourth.

I'm going to find him." Rich skulked away toward my left. I kept surveying the grounds. No sign of the last guy from the SUV. I also heard no sirens. Even though first responders wouldn't come into the house, between the fire and the shooting, I figured someone would have called the cops. Maybe this street really was empty.

On the far side of the yard past the house, Rich moved away from the burning structure and deeper into the yard. It was a mess of shrubs and overgrowth, perfect for hiding a goon who didn't mind getting dirty. Then I saw the fourth man stalking Rich with a two-by-four. "Shit," I muttered as I stood and ran. "Behind you!" I yelled, but before Rich could turn, the other guy clubbed him and sent him crashing to the ground. I pushed ahead faster as the assailant bent down to pick up Rich's gun. He grabbed it and stood. "Put it down," I said as I got to within twenty feet.

The gunman looked at me, then the prone Rich, who lay in the grass and groaned. I took a couple steps closer. My pulse thumped in my ears.

"You gonna shoot me?" he said. I recognized him from the fight at the motel, but he had been one of the guys who fought Rich.

"I will if you raise the gun." He held it in front of him, still pointed toward the earth.

"Ever shoot anyone before?" He grinned at me like a predator eying its next meal.

"First time for everything." My heart rate slowed a bit now I wasn't running, but the situation kept it high. I didn't have Rich's practiced calm. I hoped I wouldn't need it. This asshole would put Rich's firearm down, I would pistol-whip him, and it would be over.

"Sure you got it in you?" he said.

"You're close to finding out," I said. I was fifteen feet

away and a good enough shot not to miss at this distance.

He looked at Rich, then at me again. "Yeah, I guess you're right." This screamed setup, like the guy who fakes turning away and then throws a punch. I stayed on guard. The goon raised his left hand and started to crouch.

Then the gun flashed up.

I fired once. Twice. A third time.

Three red spots appeared on the man's chest, two on the left side and one on the right. He looked confused. The gun toppled from his hand. He tried to say something, but his mouth didn't work, and a thin stream of blood ran out instead.

Then he fell to his knees and pitched forward.

I dropped my own pistol and stared ahead.

I'd just killed a man.

* * *

EVERYTHING TRANSPIRED IN SLOW MOTION. Rich sat up and rubbed his head. He peered at the dead goon, then at me. His head pivoted slowly, as if he moved underwater. I kept staring ahead. It was all I could do. Rich looked down and saw the gun. He said something, but I couldn't understand it, like he shouted from behind a waterfall. Rich crouched and shook my shoulders. I blinked for the first time since I dropped the gun.

"Are you all right?" he said, and I understood it this time.

"I . . . I . . . shot him."

"Yeah. Good thing, too. I don't know how the fucker

snuck up on me. He would have shot you or me. Or both of us."

"I shot him," I said again.

Rich frowned. "First time, right?" I nodded. He sighed. "Always the worst. Look, you'll get past it. I can help you." He glanced around. "And I will. Wait there." Rich left for a short while. It could have been ten seconds or an hour. Whichever, he came back and stuffed something in his pockets. "Right now, we should go. Who knows if these assholes called for reinforcements?" He collected my .45.

I felt myself nod. What Rich said made sense. We should leave. More goons could be rolling up any minute. I knelt on the ground, unmoving, as if I'd grown roots. My legs didn't want to move. "Come on," Rich said. He hooked me under the arm and lifted me up. I stumbled in the direction of the Camaro. Rich gripped my bicep to steady me as we jogged. He opened the door and shoved me in. I stared forward and fumbled with the seatbelt. The V8's rumble broke my reverie. Rich turned the car around and took off down the street. "We have to change motels," he said as we sped along the road. "Even if we have to stay outside the city, it's worth it." He paused, obviously waiting for me to concur. I couldn't form any words, so I nodded.

Something burned in my gut. I replayed the scene over and over. The man walloped Rich with a plank. I ran toward him. He acted like he was putting the gun down, then tried to raise it. I shot him. Once. Twice. Three times. Red spread across his chest. He lay face-down in the grass. At least his dead eyes didn't stare at me. It may have been too much right now.

The burning traveled up my throat. "Pull over," I managed to say. Rich jerked the wheel and skidded the car to a stop near the treeline. I opened the door, staggered out, and vomited. I puked again and again, until I heaved only air. I closed my eyes and took a few ragged breaths. Rich put a hand on my shoulder. "You did the right thing," he said.

I nodded. On some level, I knew it. "Doesn't feel like it right now," I said in a raw, scratchy voice. Between the fire and throwing up, my throat felt like I gargled with lava.

Rich handed me a couple napkins. I was about to ask where he got them when he said, "You brought a bag of food with you?"

In spite of the situation, I chuckled. "It was in my hand when everything went down." I wiped my mouth. I wished I could have sandblasted it.

"When you're feeling up to it, go ahead and eat." He looked down at the pool of vomit in the grass and handed me a bottle of water. "I think you'll need to."

I drained half of it in one long swig. "Maybe later," I said.

"You better now?"

"Yeah." I stood. A little wobbly, but I made it.

"Let's go, then."

Again in the car, we headed headed toward Route 219. "Let's check out of the motel," Rich said when we were closer. "If it looks like someone is sitting on it, we keep going."

"I want my laptop and gear," I said. Rich glared at me. "It's good stuff. I'm not letting it go just because a couple assholes are outside our doors." We got to 219. "Make a right," I said.

"What? Why?"

"I want to see if anyone is camped out behind our

rooms. It'll work better if no one sees your super obvious car drive past the lot."

We snaked our way around the back roads, emerging onto 219 above the hotel. Rich pulled over, and I got out. "Be careful," he said.

"I'll try to leave the shooting to you," I said. I approached the motel from the rear. The rear windows of our rooms faced a grassy lot, then a short fence. I kept low, moving along the fence, but I was the only person out here. A single bound got me over the barrier. Now I hoped I picked the right room. The window in my bathroom wasn't big, but I could fit through it. First, I need it to be unlocked. Of course, it wasn't.

I owned a special keyring full of tools for picking locks, but it was inside. There didn't appear to be a way to open the window from the outside, anyway. So I improvised. I took the gun out of my pants, gripped the slide, and smashed the handle into the glass. I cleared some remaining shards. A few sharp bits remained. I doffed my sweatshirt and draped it over the bottom of the window frame. I lifted myself through the window, grunting in pain as my left shoulder barked at me again.

My feet hit the bathroom floor. I opened the door slowly, my muzzle leading the way. If anyone was in the room, they were the hide and seek world champion. I grabbed my gear and tossed it into my bag. Then I saw my clothes. I liked what I brought. There was space in the bag. I shoved everything in and walked back into the bathroom. No one waited for me outside the window. I craned my neck and looked in both directions. The area was goon-free. I threw the bag onto the grass, climbed out behind it, and dashed back to Rich's car.

* * *

I PERSUADED Rich to pull over. We got off 219 and turned into a parking lot behind a nondescript building. Someone would have to look for us to notice us here. "What are we doing?" he said. I thumbed through a few notes on my phone.

"Finding a place to stay," I said.

"We can find another motel."

"So can the people who tried to kill us."

"You have a better idea?" said Rich.

"We'll see." I found the number and called. Luke Thompson answered on the second ring. "You still want a story?"

"What do you have in mind?" he said.

I gave him a rundown of recent events. "Our concern is they're looking for us. They could have more guys, or they could even have some deputies."

"You want a place to stay." It wasn't a question.

"Plus a place to hide the most obvious car in the county for a day or two," I said. Rich frowned. I covered my phone. "I'm not the one with a bright blue Camaro."

"I think I can help you with those," said Luke.

"Thanks."

"It's not out of the kindness of my heart. I want to fill page one with the story you guys are going to give me."

"I think you'll be able to," I said. "We need a little time to wrap it up, but it could be a career-maker."

"Where are you now?" I told him. "Stay there. I'll come meet you. Then you can follow me. I'll try to keep us off the main roads as much as possible."

I hung up. We waited.

* * *

WE TRAILED Luke's Jeep along the side roads of Oakland. A couple blocks from the *Republican's* office, he led us to a body shop. Rich pulled the Camaro into a vacant bay. We got out. The door closed behind us. "My brother's shop," Luke said when we got into his Jeep Wrangler—Rich up front and me in the back. "He'll keep it in there for a couple days. Shouldn't take you longer than that, right?"

"No," Rich said. "I think we're close to wrapping it up."

"Good." Luke pulled out onto the road. "What else do you need to do?"

"Tie up loose ends," I said. "I need to do some research. There have to be connections here."

"Connections where?"

"Between Land of the Brave, the mayor, maybe the sheriff's office, and whoever provides meatheads for hire."

"I grabbed a couple of their IDs," Rich added. "Doesn't tell us who hired them, but we can still use it."

"I'll see if I can help you with it," Luke said. He steered us down yet another in a series of twisty streets I couldn't distinguish. "I've lived here long enough."

"I do . . . different research than a lot of people," I said.

"Hacking?"

I spoke to his eyes in the rearview. "None of it will be traceable back to you."

"So you're the law and order one," Luke said, inclining his head at Rich. Then he half-turned to glance at me. "And you're the one who colors outside the lines."

"I'm the better-looking one, too," I said. Rich snorted in the passenger's seat. I saw the top third of his head shaking above the headrest.

"I'll make sure the readers know," said Luke.

"Please do."

Luke owned a small, two-story house with a short driveway leading to a detached garage more like a barn. He parked the Jeep, and we all went into his home. It felt cool, like he hadn't run the heat since spring began six months ago. Ugly green carpeting covered the floors. It went with the beige walls, but it was still hideous. If my house had come with such abominable carpet, I might have burned the whole place to the ground to ensure I was rid of it.

The rest was furnished by and for a bachelor. Luke and I shared similar tastes in furniture if not in quality. The living room consisted of a sofa, recliner, entertainment center with two game consoles, and a large TV mounted on the wall. The dining room held a small square table and four plain chairs. "You can setup here for now," Luke said. He told me his Wi-Fi password. A minute later, my laptop was on his network and connected to the VPN. "You don't take many chances, do you?"

"Not with my technology," I said.

Rich and Luke adjourned to the dining room while I banged away at my research. The people were certain to be connected. The helpful mayor, the nice charity director, guys like Billy, the four goons. I couldn't link them professionally, and in a small town, I couldn't go around and interrogate people. It left Google and other tools. I preferred those to most people anyway.

There are plenty of websites, legitimate and otherwise, dedicated to aggregating information about people. With the right search parameters, you could find a trove of embarrassing information on most people. Humiliation was always nice, but I wanted to see how these people fit together. Ken Dennehy. Pete and George Russell. The two dead assholes whose wallets ended up in Rich's pocket. Even Billy the drug delivery guy. Something other than drugs tied them to each other.

The first domino fell in about a minute. George Russell took his wedding vows thirteen years ago, marrying Dawn Dennehy, sister of Ken. The siblings' older sister Sheila married a man now deceased. Their son William in West Virginia struggled with addiction and often found himself on the wrong side of the law. The dead husband, Edward Leonard, fathered a son from his first marriage. Tyler Leonard's picture looked back at me from one of the dead men's wallets. A family operation, more or less.

This would give Luke his story. He could pull a couple more threads and unravel the whole thing. I did enough of the heavy lifting for him.

Now Rich and I had to bring these people down.

CHAPTER 11

IN THE OTHER ROOM, RICH CALLED SOMEONE HE knew in the Maryland State Police. I heard him make the case for not summoning the feds—the operation was careful about state lines—and it sounded like he won the argument. He hung up and rejoined us in the living room. "State cops will be here in the morning," said Rich. "They're looping in the West Virginia boys, too, for the other side of the border.

"Why so long?" I said.

"They like to work within the law. Gotta take the case to a state's attorney and get a warrant."

"I thought you were off the clock."

"Captain Norton isn't," Rich said.

"I guess you're bunking here," Luke said. "The loft above the garage has a couple beds in it and bathroom."

"Can I borrow some clothes for tomorrow?" Rich asked me.

"I'm not sure my stuff will fit you well," I said. "Besides, you'll look way more fashionable than normal."

Luke offered to get some clothes for Rich in town. While he ran the errand, Rich and I checked out our sleeping quarters. The first thing I noticed was the brown shag carpeting. I hoped Luke didn't choose something so ghastly. With a better layout, the loft would make a functional apartment. It could hold a bedroom, bathroom, living room, and kitchen. As configured, it featured the kitchen and bathroom, and the rest of the place was undefined. Two twin beds sat close to a sofa, which was in the vicinity of an old recliner and ancient TV. With a few weekends of work, Luke could rent this place out.

Speaking of Luke, he came back about an hour later with clothes and food. We ate pizza from Tomanetti's at the dining room table. After our meal, we went over the story. Luke assembled the skeleton of it already, but he was missing a lot of bones and connective tissue. Rich and I provided those for him. He took notes on his laptop, showing off a typing rate my keyboarding instructors from middle school would have envied. "Jesus Christ," he said when we finished. I expected smoke to waft up from his laptop.

"It's a lot to take in," I said.

"They've been pretty brazen about it, too. George Russell using his own bank accounts." Luke frowned and keyed in another note. "I wonder if some of those withdrawals went to law enforcement or federal regulators."

"Maybe." I shrugged. "I figured they were for snatching a box of drugs here and there. Who knows? Maybe you can find out before the police do."

"It'd be safer to let them do it," Rich chimed in.

"Ever the wet blanket," I said.

Rich rolled his eyes. "Nosing around could be

dangerous right now. We don't know if Billy blabbed to everyone he knows. They could be wise to us."

"Which is why we're staying here."

"And why you should wait for the police," Rich said to Luke. "Type up your story and send it to your boss the second the cuffs get slapped on. But going off the reservation for a scoop could get you hurt. Or worse."

Luke took Rich's advice better than I would have—and better than I've taken whatever advice he's given me over the years. "All right," he said. "I'll write what I have and send it in. My boss will sit on it until the time is right. Then it'll go out online and in the next morning's edition."

"You have a handgun?" I said.

"It's Garrett County," Luke said. "Everyone has a handgun."

"Fair enough. Might want to bring it with you tomorrow. If Billy ran his mouth, it could get ugly."

"I've never shot anyone before," Luke said.

His words rang in my ears like the three shots I fired. I wished I could still make the same claim.

* * *

THE NEXT MORNING, Luke and I ate breakfast—he ran out to Sheetz—at his dining room table while Rich showered and put on his new clothes. He joined us a few minutes later. Rich's eye for fashion is a couple years behind and hit-and-miss, but he always picked jeans to fit perfectly. The pants he wore today did not. They were carpenter's denims with a bunch of straps to dangle tools from, and they were both too big in the waist and too long in the inseam. Rich's belt did yeoman's work to keep the pants around his midsection, while the legs were rolled into inch-high cuffs. Despite Rich's preemptive scowl, I laughed.

"Want to hang some drywall before we leave?" I said. Rich ignored me, sat at the table, and grabbed a coffee. "Maybe we could saw a bunch of two-by-fours. Is it 'measure twice, cut once'?"

"Yes," Rich said. If a hammer hung from its proper loop, his expression indicated he might have hit me with it.

"Look on the bright side," I said. "If you ever need to infiltrate the guys standing outside Home Depot, you have the perfect disguise."

Luke covered his mouth and chuckled. Rich sighed and looked through the Sheetz bag for breakfast. He pulled out a breakfast sandwich and a donut. We all finished eating, and I wished Luke came back with more coffee. A coffee maker was conspicuous by its absence in his kitchen. "Where is your friend meeting us?" Luke asked Rich.

"Land of the Brave headquarters," he said. "He'll have some state cops with him. At the same time, the West Virginia cops are going to hit the hospital and scoop up George Russell and his people."

"If it's all simultaneous, nobody can tip anyone else off," I said.

"Sometimes, the cops have good ideas, too," said Rich.

"Let's hope it all goes as planned."

After breakfast, we got in Luke's Jeep and drove toward Deep Creek Lake. "Does your state police friend know you're coming dressed like Bob Vila?" I said.

"I'm surprised you know who Bob Vila is," said Rich, ignoring the barb.

"I watch YouTube. Besides, he's part of pop culture."

"I agree," Luke said. "I was way too young for his show, but I know who he is."

"Great," Rich said, "we're all Bob Vila fans."

"Looks like you are most of all," I said.

Rich shook his head, but I saw a brief smirk pass over his face. A few minutes later, we approached Land of the Brave. The parking lot held about the same number of cars it did when Rich and I came before. "Keep going," Rich said. "They're not here yet." It didn't take long for us to encounter the state contingent. A short distance along 219, a convoy of unmarked state police cars rolled past us. Luke turned around while Rich made a phone call. He told whoever answered we were in the Jeep but declined to mention his inadvertent disguise as a carpenter.

We parked near the police cars. A couple troopers jogged to the rear of the building. Rich introduced me to Captain Casey Norton. He was about my height but broad like Rich with short blond hair and dark green eyes. The hair showed no gray, though a few creases around the eyes made me guess Norton to be about Rich's age. If the police career didn't work out, he could always try out for the Ravens as a linebacker. "Rich told me about you," he said as we shook hands.

"He embellishes a lot," I said. Rich only complimented me to his law enforcement peers after running me down first.

"Your reputation precedes you."

"Is forewarned a good thing?"

"I guess we'll find out," Norton said.

We proceeded inside, bypassing the startled receptionist and heading right to Pete Russell's office. Rich led the way. Russell smiled initially, but his expression soured when he saw the retinue of troopers walking behind Rich. "You're done, you piece of shit," he said.

"What's the meaning of this?" Russell said, standing and banging his desk.

"Peter Russell," Norton said, "you're under arrest for possession of narcotics, distribution of narcotics, theft, conspiracy to distribute narcotics, and conspiracy to commit murder."

"This is outrageous! I run a legitimate charity."

"You killed Jim Shelton," Rich said. He stood nose-to-nose with Russell. "Jim was my friend. I would love it if you'd resist arrest." Rich clenched and unclenched his hands into fists. Norton stared at him and frowned.

"If he starts beating this guy," I said to Norton, "you'll have to pull him off."

"You wouldn't?"

I shook my head. "He's an asshole. He deserves a pummeling."

"We won't let him get pounded."

"Pity," I said.

Russell didn't resist. He put his hands up. Rich stayed in his face until Norton tapped his shoulder. Only then did he relent. Norton and his troopers arrested Russell and led him outside. Rich and I followed with Luke. Back in the Jeep, I said, "I was hoping you'd hit him."

"It was tempting," said Rich. "I'm not sure I could have stopped."

"I wouldn't have pulled you off."

"Really?" Rich said.

"Really."

"I knew I brought you for a reason."

* * *

Norton and another trooper stayed behind while the rest of the convoy left with Peter Russell. He spent a couple minutes on the phone with a counterpart in West Virginia. We leaned on the Jeep and waited. When he hung up, Norton came down and talked to us. "They got the brother," he said, "plus a few other guys."

"What about the mayor?" I said.

"Being questioned. We don't know what his involvement is."

"And the sheriff?" Rich said.

Norton shrugged. "No evidence that he or his men took part," he said.

"The mayor might have ordered them around," I suggested.

"Then if it happened, it's on the mayor and those deputies."

Norton shook hands with us and departed with his fellow trooper. "You have everything you need for the story?" I said to Luke.

"I think so." He nodded. "There's a version online already. I'll add more details, and updates will go on the site later and out in the paper tomorrow morning."

"Remember us when you're a big-timer."

He smiled. "I like it at the *Republican*. This city and county are more my speed than a place like Baltimore."

"I'll look for your Pulitzer acceptance speech, then," I said.

"I'll start drafting it tomorrow," Luke said. He drove us back to his house, where we picked up our stuff before going to his brother's garage to get Rich's car.

From there, we stopped at the motel. The fellow behind the desk wanted to charge us for another night, but a look at Rich's badge and glare changed his mind. We collected Rich's things and pulled onto 219. He drove to the Shelton house. I waited in the car while he talked to Connie at the door. They chatted for a few minutes. Connie's head bowed, and her shoulders shook. Rich hugged her while she cried on his shoulder. After the tears passed, they talked for another minute and embraced again.

Rich got back in the car. "I think they'll be OK," he said.

"Good. What about money?"

"I'm sure they'll sue Russell for wrongful death, if nothing else."

"You know," I said, "I could get back into his bank records. It would only take a few minutes to reallocate some of his money."

"No," Rich said. "The state police are all over this. We can't have an irregularity now."

"OK."

"You understand?"

"Not really," I said, "but I'll go along to get along." I paused. "Did you tell her?"

"Tell her what?"

"Why Jim died."

Rich remained quiet for a few seconds before he said, "I think she already knew he figured something out. They both wanted to believe Land of the Brave was doing good for the right reasons." He sighed. "Jim was always curious and smart. We used to tell him he'd make a good MP."

"Did he take it as a compliment?"

"We didn't really mean it as one," Rich said with a

small smile. "We were infantry. Didn't have a lot of use for military cops."

"Yet you basically traded one uniform for another," I pointed out.

"I think Jim could have, too."

"Luke said he's going to mention Jim putting the drug angle together in his piece."

"Good. You convinced him it was worth it?" I inclined my head. "Thanks." Rich pulled out of the neighborhood. A couple minutes later, we turned onto 219 to start the drive back home.

* * *

THE NEXT MORNING, I got the call I expected. "Hi, Mom."

"Coningsby, your father and I read what you and Richard did in Garrett County," she said. Yes, Coningsby is my real first name. It's from family on my mother's side. Why I go by my initials is obvious. The fact my mother insists on not using them is annoying.

"Don't tell me you read a newspaper called the *Republican*," I said. "You'll be a pariah at the rotary club."

"The *Sun* picked up the story, dear. No one at the rotary club will know."

"What a relief."

"I'm not sure I like the idea of Richard recruiting you," my mother said. "I know he did it for his friend's family, so I guess the right people got the help they needed in the end."

"They did," I said.

"And you brought that awful organization down."

"It's a shame. Land of the Brave started out doing

good work. I wish they'd simply stuck with it. They could have helped a lot of people."

"Maybe someone will try again," she said. I wondered if my parents' foundation would look for opportunities in Garrett County. It was the kind of thing they would do.

"Maybe they will."

"Your father and I will draft you a paycheck later today. Good work, Coningsby."

"Thanks, Mom," I said.

"Make sure you call Gloria. She's a nice girl."

"I will."

We hung up. A few other calls came in. I ignored them. An article like the one in the Sun always spiked my inquiries in the short term. Most of them could be safely dismissed. I didn't want to take a new case now, anyway. My shoulder and back still hurt from falling through the carport and having the ceiling collapse on me. I would need a few days to recover physically—and following the shooting, maybe longer to recover mentally.

I pushed the memory out of my mind and texted Gloria.

Hi! Thanks for reading this novella. I hope you enjoyed reading it as much as I did writing it.

Here are the other books in my catalog:

The C.T. Ferguson Crime Novels:

1. The Reluctant Detective
2. The Unknown Devil
3. The Workers of Iniquity
4. Already Guilty
5. Daughters and Sons
6. A March from Innocence
7. Inside Cut
8. The Next Girl
9. In the Blood
10. Right as Rain
11. Dead Cat Bounce (December 2021)

The C.T. Ferguson Crime Novellas:

1. The Confessional (book 1.5 in overall series continuity)
2. Land of the Brave (2.5)
3. Red City Blues (3.5)
4. Blood on Canvas (8.5)

The John Tyler Action Thrillers

1. The Mechanic
2. White Lines
3. Lost Highway
4. Four on the Floor (Spring 2022)

While these are the suggested reading sequences, each novel is a standalone mystery or thriller, and the books can be enjoyed in whatever order you happen upon them.

Do you like free books? You can get the prequel novella to the C.T. Ferguson mystery series for free. *Hong Kong Dangerous* is unavailable for sale and is exclusive to my readers. Visit https://www.subscribepage.com/hkd2020 to get your book!

Connect with me:

For the many ways of finding and reaching me online, please visit https://tomfowlerwrites.com/contact. I'm always happy to talk to readers.

This is a work of fiction. Characters and places are either fictitious or used in a fictitious manner.

"Self-publishing" is something of a misnomer. This book would not have been possible without the contributions of many people.

- The great cover design team at 100 Covers.
- My editor extraordinaire, Chase Nottingham.
- My wonderful advance reader team, the Fell Street Irregulars.

* 9 7 9 8 2 0 1 6 1 7 4 0 0 *